I0579830

Talking Man

Lynn Miller

Talking Man

Copyright 2017 Lynn Miller

This book is a work of fiction. Names, characters, places and incidents either are products of the author's imagination or are used fictitiously. Any resemblance to actual events or locales or persons living, or dead, is entirely coincidental.
That's what the attorneys advise we say. But then there is the twisted humor of it; if it be fiction it is, afterall, an amalgam of lies. If the author thus be a comsummate liar, can we trust him to tell us if any of it be true? If it be thin fiction, where hides the deniability?

First Edition
Davila Art & Books
PO Box 1404
Sisters, Oregon 97759
541-549-0817

www.lynnrmiller.com

ISBN 978-1-885210-21-0

The cover photo is by the author. It is of a porcelain faucet as modified Model T radiator cap allowing a manually adjustable pressure release.

table of contents

Predilection

Orientation

An Inclined Plane

"Any offer will be rewarded."

"He means to say 'don't make an offer unless you want it'."

"I don't understand."

"Okay, understand this - go away now and when the drugs wear off, we'll try again."

"I'm not on any drugs. What are you talking about?"

"Leave now, you are wasting my time, and it hurts me to watch life pass you by."

"But I want it. And you are the problem because you have it priced too high."

"What sort of lilly-livered bastard needs everything

handed to him on a platter?"

"God you're weird. I think you're afraid to say out loud, straight out, what you want for that."

When the chair hit him it broke into pieces as did the young man's left knee - shattered. He took the small pistol out of his pocket and shot the first old man dead. Then he tossed the pistol to the second old man and said, "Now he no longer has to watch life pass me by."

"You're the loser, young man, because now you will never know how cheaply you might have bought it."

Whole damn curtain drops, rod, rope and all.

Up

Passing through prisms of wet reflection with neon peripheries, we entered that Paris alley hung as it was like New Orleans in layers of fine April rain. The sign said Bouillon Chartier, a soup kitchen for locals. Butcher paper covering small tables, cigarette smoke as though dispersed by a moisturizer. I set down my camera and tape recorder, opened the small satchel and retrieved the watercolor travel pack and postcard-sized water color paper. JC, opposite me, held his curious smile in respectful check.

I took photos in every direction, turned the little tape recorder on and placed it in the center of the table. Before the waiter shuffled over, Jean raised his eyebrows towards my pile...

"We won't be here very long. This is my way to burn this meal, this place, into my brain. A sound track, photos, a quick water color sketch or two, notes in my journal especially of the meal. It is my way to make time slow down - to stretch it out - to bend it to my will, if only slightly."

The waiter stood over us disdainfully, pencil in hand. I asked for a coffee which instantly irked him. He twitched. Jean squeezed the waiter still with his eyes and with his muttering of a long insult in French.

The waiter, head up on slack body, then wrote what we ordered in a scribble directly on that paper table cloth and spun to go, advertising his low regard of me and, in his missed step, his fear of his countryman.

JC offered. "It was because for him cappucino is an after-dinner desert. His comfort comes of believing there is a right and wrong way. Forgive him, he is a pig."

To my palette the food was simple and excellent - but much of that because it was new and fresh. Ignorant pleasure.

A glass of water, paints open, and brushes at the ready I felt the dark walls disappear and the tables and fronts of people glow. The meals gave off their own light. I reached with my eyes for small sights and allowed them to flow through my brain to my fingers and out the brush hairs to the coarse paper.

Eating, talking, looking, painting, making notes, allowing the tape recorder to capture wider ambient sound, taking photos - that short hour was crammed so full it became many hours in my 'enhanced' memory. It became many visits, not just the one. It become a frenzy inside a calm that was plan or the result of one. I was a young old man, an absorbent instrument in my actual time. I was deep inside the Talking Man, mute as a jumping bean.

The word pictures, the pictured words, spill out constantly. Before; the game included an effort to mold the pieces of the spillage to some project, effort or grand entry. Hide the fear, cloak it from myself. At all costs, hold on to the appearance of clarity. Alone clarity is a crutch without which the terror would make of me the whimpering coward I wait to be. With others clarity is the seemingly well chosen attire that announces an intelligent pattern.

I want to be with others just so long as the masquerade is allowed. I need to be the one who cares, who gives, who absorbs the pain, who deflects the blows, who hovers above beautiful in appropriate abandon. I want to be seen as clarity and pattern.

Then it swivels, half turn to the right, it swivels and with the gaping audience I wonder after my crazy turnabout. I am sickened by others, they remind me of myself, my weaknesses, my deadened soul, my lapses to naugahyde lethargy, my perfumed stench, my dog food speech, my ugly beauty, my sharp-edged nose hairs, my seed-filled half-rolled cuffs, my rotting toe nails, my sameness. My I. My me.

Alone, there is a chance that artificial romance will swallow the me - the I. It comes to this, presumptions have failed, the spillage roars and demands shape presumption would fear. The words want out. They screech against molds, they chew on each other for lack of the conclusive mathematical design painted only out of freedom. The words chose me, perhaps because I am riddled with the perforations of inadequacy, or perhaps there was a need for that humor only a squealing squirrel or rat dare lend a dead-end life.

Anecdotal life as a governable social tool would demand the simplistic linear. Start with the irrefutable, end with unreconciliable. Society would deflate and demean all evidence of complexity in a life, in a living, in a community of living. The notion that a full life be shaped, conclusively by a simple early defining moment of terror, loss, love and/or joy is quintessentially republican and moronic. "Republican" by classic definition would be the assignation to a handful of representatives, of social design, legitimacy, purpose and future. The representatives must satisify all notions of representation which means that ideas and their connective tissue must pass through a colander with one single slightly plugged hole. Pulp-free, colorless, sterile rationale.

At thirteen years of age the terrors are juvenile. At nineteen years of age the terrors are desperate. Six short years and one of the slowest periods in a life. Short time, long time. The impetus, or lack of it starts here. Be out ahead of yourself? Or follow yourself in cautiously, until experience cools and coats. Or wait for it to dump on you. Youth is wasted on the secure. Just as exhiliration is wasted on the well-dressed, recently-washed, rule-following, thumb-sucking, proud-praying apologists. Forgive them Lord, they aren't capable of feeling a damn thing.

Give me a two-ply sadness! Give me an undercoated laugh! Give me a low-hanging hopefulness! Give me a suds-free friendship! Give me an edible furniture polish! Give me a break!

Keep 'em. I don't want your stinking gifts. My fingers are as clean as I need them to be. My immune system is putrid with beneficial bugs and that is as it should be.

There are no doors. Not in any traditional sense. Where the walls appear to meet at corners there are gaps available to peer through or exit. All the windows are spinning mirrors. The bottoms of the walls are embroidered with lacey patterns. The dark man in attendance is mute and refuses to acknowledge us. Tiny running horses the size of earwigs, make a noise like the slicing of water.

Recollection. Re-collect. It works for me, in my brain, in my lost self, in my next self, because what happens today triggers the recollection - the re-collecting. No one else can know how. But that doesn't matter. What matters is that the place it all comes from and the places it all goes belong to a universal math of consciousness, a patterning, that everyone recognizes as "that place".

Midnight. Slept one hour, then wide awake. Took a sleeping pill, didn't work. It wasn't fear or worry which woke me this time. Perhaps heat. One hundred today. Have been soaking two face towels in cold water and draping them over the pillow. There is a small shock when I first rest my head on the cold wetness but it is immediately replaced by great relieving comfort. Within a few minutes the heat of my head, of my brain, turns the wet clothes warm. And I must rotate them. This process until I fall asleep. I have no fever, no temperature to the touch. It is as if the heat is an action or reaction - rather than a condition. Perhaps the summer itself? Listened to a passage in Tchiakovsky, piano and strings piece, which reproduced this heat transfer in tone - and the music seemed to offer that the condition would morph to other sweeps and cadence. Or was it the structured travelling pathos of a Dvorak string quartet, without narrative arc, all carriage and the woods in hollows forbading pause? Oh, the illusive heat of my head.

The word picture, the pictured words. The talking language. The talking man. Walk away from him and the talking will follow you, separate from him and follow you. The talking is separate from the man. The man is NOT separate from the talking.

Eleven years old and in a daze of sleep deprivation. Air conditioning was for the very rich. Still nights at 85 degrees, thick with sweat and decaying appetites. Unless it was the black-haired indifferent girl, the one with the "I could eat you up and spit you out and not feel a thing." You hunger for a lingering look and a kind word from her, instead you feel her superiority. "You will never know how delicious it is to see you as the useless worm you are." Her messages bounce off the Loquat and Eucalyptus leaves in their heat-seeking race to kill you.

Kill me, over and over again. No rebirthing in this process, all cataclysm, all wrenching and interupted nightmare. Magnetic force swirls in, directly, with the bolt upright 'Oh No!' slap awakes. The magnetic force eases the terror and draws you, me, towards visions of the black-haired indifferent girl. Stupid, low, thin. Eleven years old and a slave to desire, to heat-thick casement, to sweet sick debasement. That was 47 years ago, when emotions had the space and environment to swell and burst; when starch shirts and protruding ears lent a calcified counterpoint to tropical hungers; when future meant opportunity; when migratory birds could, for the most part, trust their genetic memory.

The black-haired indifferent girl smiles the clear sweet spiderless smile which says "come here - smile at me the way I smile at you. Hold me just with your smile. Let our smiles wrap around each other. Please, now, quick." And in that glorious moment her indifference, that crippling disregard, is gone. You, I, we fall to our kness happy, muttering that we always knew it could be like this. And a black sheet falls from somewhere as we see her loveliness tranform back into the cruel indifference activated by a cackling laugh of rejection.

And I'm not eleven years old anymore. I'm fifty something and it's a world of seams, quilt-like, but with the awkwardness of a broken non-rhyming pattern. There are canyons and blind-spots where perceptions ought to join but don't. There are overlaps which don't exactly line up. And when I let go of my old insistence, I feel the poetry. But that can't last long. It's the predictability that destroys the attraction. Poetry is ultimately reciteable. Say it often enough and the screams start in. Stop it! That's enough! It's all too much pretty speech. The music in patterning of words, phrases, metaphors, illusions, always faces the risk of excusable recognition, of marketability, of propaganda, of obvious package.

Human invention versus the correct dynamics of natural design. They fight to some odd causes and the exchange frequently results in strong possibilities for timeless beauty. The plastic against the passionate, the geometric against the loving, the dry skin and the wet.

What can anyone say? If the future doesn't belong to correctness, deliberation, order, or form then how are we to plan our moves, our meals, our clothing, our breeding choices? Some live a soft-covered life without insistence, without slip covers, wholly controlled by angry editors. While a few live hard-covered lives full of footnotes, postscripts, addendums, bent corners, underlinings, and bulk. Angry, silly comparisons as far from understanding as youth is from the young.

When loneliness contorts towards a vacuum and the same green looks different, whatever falls near the hole takes the shape desired by lonely, desired by crippled, demanded by allegorical inertia. Bricks are made of those lies, bricks of gas and decay. The construct begins in the beginning to fall in on itself, and the most unfortunate leaning denies ascendancy. At the top, or the projected top, the weight loads the snare. Up, then down, spring-loaded in a painful arch, tethered to the ground - ready to snap and lift. Every well-set snare began as contorted vacuum. And that contorted vacuum is the passionate opposite of Pascal's Triangle where each position has its mathematical determinate all pointing to the middle. The cool future belongs to Pascal's Triangle. The vacuum snare makes a case for a futureless future. The mathematician/philosopher in the snare by an ankle figures the amortization on used futures.

No it wasn't like that. And as for the present, body chemistry cloaks the truth. How are we to know from the inside, if selfless generosity is strength or weakness? If it is truly selfless it comes from, and reinforces, a painful loneliness. And when we find companionship and the loneliness subsides, it never completely goes, it remains in a dusty pocket of our soul. Remains ready to catapult tragic loss to totemic proportions and form all symbols, stacked one on top of another, clothed in moss, denying laughter, struggling to give poetry to inescapable pain and rain.

I write these words with no traditional goal or purpose, no proposed publication, no visualized audience. I write these words, I say these words, as tho it were a bleeding. From a short distance I know I need the coagulative properties of humor, of project work, of love's distractions, of the needs of another.

We do choose our words and our posture for different company, different ears, different needs. With a goal of communicating the procedures required for successful outcome, we go from A to B. With the goal of winning attention of another human person we go from smile of recognition to look of wonder. So, when the audience is the wound, the bleeding wound, and the words are the blood, our behavioral filters are useless. It is not that caution is useless. It is that form comes from the knocking rhythms of ping ponging word balls in the hollow head. We need a word here, a turning, lifting phrase here, a tapping laundry list here. Ah, that's right, we've found a beat!

Does the beat require a story, a ballad, a purpose above itself? If countenance rises above and spiritualizes form, is beat implied, accelerated, accentuated, aggravated, lifting, pushing hum? Is beat a lasting factor or a string to pull with? In death does the beat remain? Countenance remains, glowing and caressing memories and purpose. Beat threatens to remain. And threats seem to come out of tempo, at odd hesitations, when the 'thing' would insert itself in the conveyor movement of inevitability. Threats destroy beat.

Ideas always as though they mattered. I am flung into the riddling spaces between spaces where the names of things and the reasonings are but dust particles. There, inside of nothing I feel the absurdity of the zen trance, of the self-hypnotic state, of the empty. It is the final joke test-flight.

I am attracted to brilliance, to demonstrations of powerful thought. It is a paradox. I am most attracted to that which I can only barely understand. It feels as though these unattainables lift me up, hold me against the wind of my great punishments. I have done crime against myself, repeatedly, in the knowledge that I lay a minefield before me. It is from this self-destructive nature that I reach for understanding of the brilliant evidence of the efforts of others, the hopeful purpose of others. I would own it as one owns a great painting: never capable of complete internal understanding but sucking strength from its poetry and evidence of buried light.

The feared road's end may be the start. Manifest expectancy. Stepping up onto the shoulders of the craggy lofty examples, those lived lives that stand as measuring sticks. I do look far ahead to the moundings of a good time's products, to my own cragginess and example. It may be the lying self-deluding mirage but its effect is quenching and exhilirating. It comes down to or up to the welcome platform thought: I have work to do, work I desire.

a.

Ages are delineated by the distance between meals. When young, the time from one of three meals a day seemed forever. With maturity, the distance between one of two meals seemed grotesquely significant. Now one meal a day crowds itself to labor.

b.

I am exhausted. I am exhausted by my schizophrenia. I am tired by the discovery that I am someone else. I don't want to fight the discovery that my best work came from the dedicated silliness of regular work, to find that I am a poor man's journalist and not a poet, an illustrator and not a painter, a property manager and not a farmer, a friend more than a father and husband, a sad joke rather than an example. I am exhausted.

The emotion is powerful and molding, pressing me towards a simple regimentation for the sake of future. If I have no future... I continued the patterns working on the plans for so long that my emptiness escapes me. Exhausted.

Do the work for the working and the little visions of possibilities. Leave the larger view to those well-fed moments of excess. Product is often waste. The religiosity is the working.

We may be inside of now. Or we may be inside of yesterday or tomorrow or imagined realms. I have been frequently inside the imagined. I'm working to find my way inside of now.

c.

Notches. If the soul has eyes, if the soul may at times look out and receive burning imprint from that which is seen, the eyes of this soul suffer from moon blindness. A floating cloud of shape-shifting fog dances inside the fluid of my soul's eye, offering occasional clarity, occasional confusion, and frequent challenge. This, when added to the sad social inadequacy of an untenable personality, would perhaps explain ridiculous, reclusive behaviors and the regular tendency to mark things complete before completion.

Do we have, ever, the opportunity to manage ourselves better? Good humor and regenerative motivation requires it. Do we search for a cure to the moonblindness or work to understand it to advantage? I suspect that an answer resides within notions of maintenance rather than the rush of adventure.

d.

The edges of perceptions and assessments may be sharp, fuzzy, watery, jagged, interlocking, and/or overlapping. Looking back over the mindscape of the assumptive and reflective, sense may be made of pattern perhaps only by use of the smudge tool, rubbing the edges sufficiently to cause the suggestion of less, or of non-chalance.

e.

A face, mishappened by a cavity which has each eye tilted toward the other, seems to float in hesitation doubting attraction, doubting rescue, doubting consumation.

A face angry with its lingering youth, demands linkage, connection, unwavering devotion.

The two faces would seem to be inseparable. Will they heal each other?

f.

The talking man listens to the stew of words which buzz around him and inside of him. Each word is a flashing light set off by ideas, memories, and visitations. They flip switches. Each word is but a clue of a piece of significance.

The talking man subdues the harangue of words by talking. While his mind and mouth and pen hand move, the buzz moves to murmur. There is no complete quiet for the talking man. There is possibilitiy for comfort and relief but it would depend on self-control and little manipulations. All of it is of the individual. No chemistry, fabrication, mass-produced self-help instruments, franchises, or fashion will democratize this peculiar if not unique manifestation of spiritual incontinence.

The talking man wets himself with ideas and seeks fanciful constructs to present and house the multi-floral embarrassments. He is not building a resume or beneficial biography. He is invoicing himself.

Where we have been, where we want to go and where we are - each may be a skeleton upon which words and word pictures are hung. For the talking man there is a fourth dimension which isn't dependent on place in the time of the mind. It is rather about place-ment. Care must be taken not to mistake "placement" with commercial notions of spirituality. The talking man is a no priest, no soothsayer, no pulpit-banging solace salesman. The talking man is a self-collared gardener of beneficial decay. Observations create winds of thought, waves of remembered odors and the chance for expand-ing diversion. They test the pagination of the larger, ultimate final story. The story we only know by adding futures, multiplying by manifest depravities, dividing by measureable innocence and adjust-ing for absurdity.

Who decides what to denote as the beginning? The talking man does. Who is capable of narrating the end? The talking man. Who fills in the between? Any and all might. If the talking man did the middle, every death, prescribed or not, would be accompanied by a soul draining prayer. Every birth would be viewed with guarded optimisn. Every sadness would be tested by inappropriate laughter, every idea rolled in manure and shot from a cannon up against the illumined protectorate of all theologies. Socratic oathes would bend the lines of new geometries resulting in prayer robes, Reggae in their singing design.

And all of that is off in the distance, away from the grotesque in-humanities, the new wars, the pestilence, the beheadings, corporate poisonings, the piles of bodies growing daily from hunger and casual

murder. And all of that is off in the distance away from the rape
and poisoning of the earth and our cohabitants. We grant sanction,
we murderous sloth, we grant sanctions to the mothers of greed,
thoughtlessness, and fortfeiture. Our reward is deniability. We don't
have to see the children gasp their last breaths, we don't have to
smell the dying earth, we don't have to dress the oozing wounds we
caused by default. We safe, we proud, we vulgar few.

Except for the talking man. His is a permanent living hell with
but the thread of respite. His today stretches beyond his end in the
salvation of reckless creativity, formal abandon, scripted filagreed
anarchy, diaphonous encrusted apologies, and helpless sugared
impulse. He is a mess with purpose, a possible designee, a likely
candidate, a fool for love, an emotional time bomb, a coat hanger.

g.

They are simple men, we are simple men. Defined by working
and colored by the spaces betwixt.

Slumped, tired, in the throwaway naugahyde chair, enshrouded
by the soft lost light of dusk, the young old man floated chosen
words towards the four old young men. Their leanings forward,
sticky with the need to hear, shaped a huddle of delicacy. How, they
had to wonder, could the slickest thickest man alive be talking this
way? Talking of endings, terminations, disruptive passage, selling
out, moving on, ripping up, dismissal, kaput, at the very least there
needed to be a hand off or a transition team, an election, a succes-
sor. Who would be the new offending tender? Here they were being
offered a preface to a memoir with no "me" in it.

g.2

Long strides, single file, across the cross walk. This is the way he ordered them to move. They needed more information. He attempted to satisfy the need by alluding to unnecessary pressures, by moving slowly around the false motive until it became prey.

"I am tired." He said, slowly. They, each of them, nodded almost imperceptively.

"I could stay here and farm these fields, as I once did. Stay here and be perfectly happy. No more runs to the office, no more phone calls, no more worrying about money, no more payrolls, no more planning, no more monitoring, no more more. I could quit travelling to speak, to do workshops, to sell."

"Doesn't it scare you to get up in front of people and talk?"

"No, it doesn't, never has. Maybe it's because I feel as though I am forever in the skin of one who has been robbed, stripped, violated. Nothing more can be done to me now, and I have something to say. Something you <u>will</u> listen to. I am not worried that you ask me to leave. You did that long ago and I left. I have not returned. I may never return, you will be coming to me when I speak and we will both feel a combination of exhiliration and disappointment."

It's not that I want out. I want to be left behind. I want marginalization. I want a single thread hem-line and genuine rust.

Concrete substance: cloth, iron, thread, water, sunlight, needle, air, elements - elemental physics, intention. Feelings abrade, emotions coagulate, sentiment sloshes, the word pictures don't work. Specificity is a draw string, a shrinking elastic band, a microwave of crisp overdone. Yet allusion is not the answer, nor is illusion. Maybe specificity is a top layer under which details lurk. Details which defy the shorthand of an apologetic maturity.

We are so clever, so sickeningly clever. So many blankets. The stack is heavy.

Writing in the early morning some feel accesses fresh clarity. The Talking Man doesn't care. The words have to come out, like eggs from a hen. When they come out light can shine or not, the Talking Man doesn't care. It's all Ohio to him. What does matter are the momentary apprehensions. Is a word coming? Now? Is one stuck sideways in the brain? Will moist fingers release the word? Will unexpected smiles slap the word aside? Will soapy water float the word? These are the things the Talking Man cares about. Questions that walk on all fours, barking in Calypso rhythm.

"Yes, sir." the black-haired blonde nurse said with a decal for a smile. "You must take this medication. You need your sleep. Nobody can sit here talking and writing non-stop for days on end. You must eat and sleep or you'll get very sick. If you don't take this liquid the Doctor will feed you through a needle and he'll make you sleep the same way. Now you don't want that, do you?"

It takes a sideways movement to conceal intent and results but it is worth it to keep the mind on this edge. She thinks I took the liquid. I think she is limited. The doctor thinks my outpouring is the result of a chemical imbalance brought on by delayed grief, stress, guilt, inadequacy, terror and spiritual indecency. He cannot accept me as I will become, he cannot see me in transit, self propelled through the constant gaseous express out my tail end. He says,

"Without self-control you are a freak show, you're unbankable. You won't be invited over to anyone's house. Your family is already asking me to give them acceptable ways to explain you to the world. They want a disease with an exotic name and terrible outcome -

blindness, rotting flesh, spasms, diarhea, death - so that their embar-
rasement might be replaced by the receipt of suitable sympathies.
And I, a doctor, have to tell them that your problem is of your own
design. That you have made yourself sick. And that the primary
symptoms are sleeplessness, lack of appetite and the fact that you
won't shut up!"

I make the observation that my doctor is selfish but not in any
"bankable" fashion. His personaility rivals linoleum, and the thing
I say which makes his eyes squint; I say, "you're heading where I am
only I got there first and I'm going quite a piece further."

The doctor writes a prescription, reads it, wads it up and throws
it away. There is release in that observed exercise, it is as if he created
something of value - deemed it currency - and disposed of it to feel
his power. He tires me.

I think of the young hunters high in the mountain wilderness.
The looks on their faces when they met the truck for supplies and
news of the world.

"Are you ready to come back out?"

"We're tired and our pants don't fit but we want to stay up here.
This is what we came for."

h.

I am all about fear. Fear and discomfiture. Cross-legged, knee
grabbing, tight throated fear. And it has become part of me. I dribble fear as an apprehensive basketball player dribbles his ball. When
the blows to the head or gut don't come, I get cocky, shift my feet
and dribble from one hand to the other. I know it won't last. The
ball will be stolen along with my protective rhythm. After which no

one will care about me.

My best moments have always been when I successfully balanced fear. When I made friends. When I kept friends. When I held myself in check.

How small and tight a ring have I drawn around myself and talking? My words, my talking constrict. The deeper I go inside my self the thinner the ideas, the more fragile the thoughts. While with my painting, when I dig into the observed, even with abstraction, the rewards are frequently graced with depth, complexity and humor. When I go deep inside myself, honoring impulse and scar tissue the results are often leaden and predictable.

The larger question in this comparison asks who chooses which? What is the purpose of pushing one result ahead of the other? If it is true that the only purpose of a writing such as this is process and release, an argument must be made for including both in ample measure for the anecdotal will sustain and fertilize the dark questionings.

The stories told prevent absolutes. I am all about fear but I am also all about embraced contradiction. I am, when given the ooze, all about humor. I am, in good company, about charity. I am when witness to cruelty all about sacrifice. I am, in darnest depravity, all about self. I am my own cancellation.

i.

When I was a young man I had been profoudly influenced by F. Montaigne's insistance, "call no man happy before his death." As a mature man of waning virtue, it is illuminating to discover that the very same words came from Simonides 2500 years ago. And he in turn was quoting the Athenian legislator Solon.

Today I read that Kierkegaard said, "Despair is sin." And I instantly think of Camus' words (or was it Ravel's?) "No daring is fatal." What does it take to fight despair? Outlook. Looking beyond, projecting to a possible or fanciful outcome. And that's where the daring comes in. It's scary, and it feels unnatural and ridiculous to be a militant optimist. It requires daring. Despair can be fatal. Daring, in and of itself, cannot.

j.

There is a threat that I will become clear to myself. A threat because if I am able to muster hope it may be from a soup of delusions which has kept targets near. As a coward I pad my sense of self with excessive performance in those aspects which do not threaten me. I avoid true external measure. No scales, no competitions, no submissions, no memberships. When I am judged and found lacking I move sideways in denial and hiding. Just to admit this strikes terror in my soul. Simple strong arguments may be made to flag away the losses, the rejection slips, the weight warnings. History stinks with the rotting pile of rejections and worse which have been piled on our best creative efforts. Songs have been written of the honor of rejection.

Definitions have swelled by the shredded battlements of society's guillotine of envy and misunderstanding. So to hide from the stoning results in a dubious self preservation clouding subsequent creativity. To stand for the rejections and the stonings may serve to restore vision, restore ownership, restore courage. The stones will fall short, the rejections make excellent toilet wallpaper. And earned clarity may be the best end.

k.

Back to the first longings, those thickest with oddly enchanting odor, temperature, sound and light. The thick red highlights
of the black-haired girl's reaching look-away from me, always away
from me. I was confined with my new "almost' in an emotional
paddock. She was weightless and hovering with old delusions, old
promises, old loss. She never saw me least of all when the laughing
thin blonde winked me away to those magic weeks of good humor.
The black-haired girl branded my insides forever. The laughing
thin blonde pulled me along at great speed and cut me loose on a
corner. It was years before I realized I had not been weaned, not
been weaned because I'd not been nursed. Rather than being raised,
nurtured, cared for - I had simply been allowed to survive. Now it
is an observation worthless in its essense. To have survived meant
nothing. To nurture means something. To create means everything.

l.

In this time of bankable adorned cynicism, the lyricists must
hide their filagreed truths. This is no time for poetic clairvoyance.
We enter a new darker age where enlightenment is punishable by
banishment at the least. An age where internment and or execution
are guaranteed those who speak of romance and adoration, who
speak of a justice of the heart, who murmur of the vulgarities of the
new communisim, who sneeze at thin spirits, who lob slow pitches
towards the childish, who worship hope and urinate on convenience, who constantly question the implied authorities of science,
who scream that the market-place should never be used as a mea-

surement of value - beauty - truth - fairness - suitability or future designs, who talk about the marketplace as the wasteland no better than the battlefields, who sob as they try to gather us unto the lesser amongst us, who laugh at our desparate selfishness. We are in a time where enlightenment has been set aside as unnecessary and bothersome, odd and irksome, untenable for a selfish ownership society. It has been replaced by the dark uncertainties of scientific and technological advance. Enlightenment, or our flirtation with it, has functioned as our spiritual and moral compass. The compass is missing now.

m.

The coffee is ready, outside a paper thin morning light skitters over the Fall frost. My old black horse will die soon. I refuse to mark time with the observation or unforgivable anxieties. Life does not belong to designations or the designee. My old black horse is neither old nor black in the molecular mosaic of life. She neither marks time nor is marked by time. My impending sadness from the loss of her will have no molecular weight unless it causes me to create something in her memory. Such an action would add to life. Of course all creativity owes some debt to the experiences of creators. It is when we refuse the unrefuteable that we flirt with a substantive hope or a cancerous denial.

n.

Today they say we must be either red or blue. No other color is acceptable. And "they" are the proudest possessors of red or blue sentiments, philosophies, attitudes, rectitudes, and polotik or polotique.

I am off-white or perhaps grey, I say.

They say "Impossible."

I say "you are not the one to designate."

"Of course that's right. But it is a war, a deadly war, and your best chance is to belong to one or the other. Otherwise you are expendable civilian collateral, fodder, cordwood, discard."

"What if I should decide to work both sides? Not as a spy but as a man of convenience and comfort, as a coward, as a realist?"

"Do you really believe you are clever enough to avoid both firing squads?"

"I have friends who say they are going to move away, to New Zealand, to Scotland. It is all too depressing and senseless and endless to them. They say they are done with this new facism. What do you say to them? How are they different from those of us who refuse to choose sides?"

"Stupid question. They are different because they choose to run-away. Our advice to them would be to stop talking about it and go, go before they are found out and tried as treasonous."

"Treasonous? How do you see it as treasonous that one would chose to live elsewhere, even it if is because of an announced disgust with the political condition?"

"If you aren't with us you are against us. It has come to this. And if you are against us you are an agent of destruction against the country: treason."

"I am not with you. I am not working against you, not yet anyway. And I refuse your notion that this would suggest I am treasonous."

"You are a suicidal fool, You don't see that these are both terrible and wonderful times. Terrible as we are surrounded by evil, wonderful because we are building a new moral ownership society - one which understands that government's primary edict is for the protection of private property. Our enemies would tear down what we have built. They would replace it with a godless socialism. We can spare no expense in our efforts to hit this enemy before it hits us. It is your determination against ours that you are no enemy. Moments after we officialize our determination, your time remaining will be in proportion to either your effectiveness or our whim. We have nothing further to discuss."

Next it will be the gestapo, the marines, the IRS, the building inspectors, the school principals, the CIA, the FBI, the narcos, the Cuban Republicans. And I live back over my lifetime thankful in tremors that I have been spared the moment or moments yet to come when the narrative is cut off by breaking glass, screaming orders, and death.

If there is to be a better next, it will come of the fabric woven from threads of humor, poetry, sacrifice, beauty, love and irreverance. The rest is memory of clouted disfiguring blood.

It is time to call for a third army. The army of interruption, the army of deliberate confusion, the army of social workers and volunteer handy men, the army of the intractibles, the army of side stepping - singing - flinging humiliators, the army which will execute the executioner and the signatories of death warrants including, in the end, themselves. The army of the grey and off-white.

o.

A revelation! The earliest boule was made from nails that were hammered into a boxwood spherical core. The nail heads so tightly packed formed a ball the skin of which resembled an iron fish.

p.

The sculptor Anthony Caro makes and states absolute rules or laws of sculpture then proceeds to artfully break them.

q.

I was nineteen, perpetually frightened and constantly squirming my way straight ahead, into and past my fears. It showed.

He was probably 35, six foot six, strong as an ox, blonde, travelling salesman in suit and top coat, and packing a well-formed death wish. Animal intelligence, drank like a pool vacuum, went from laughter to tears to blue mean, all in seconds. At war with his complete and throbbing inadequacy.

First time I saw him he was battling a San Francisco Chronicle newspaper dispenser chained to a light post. He slugged it, picked it up and threw it to the end of the chain, and it bounced back catching his leg and tearing his top coat. I, fool child, confused by what I had seen, walked up to offer help. He pushed me away then grabbed at my coat sleeve, holding me near, he still managed to free himself from the metal stand and smash in the glass front.

"Let's go get a drink." He said. I told him I was underage. He cussed and insisted I go with him, dragging me to a Sunset District Club.

1966, cold foggy, clammy San Francisco nite. The club bouncer stopped us to ask for I.D. He let go of me and hit the bouncer square in the face. First time I had ever seen such a thing. My insides fell as I backed away. He grabbed my sleeve again to yard me into the bar, not noticing the three men who came running out. For the first few minutes it seemed he had the upper hand. Then it all turned and he seemed to exhaust. They held him up and kept hitting him until he was out, completely senseless. Two of them drug him by his feet to behind a neighboring stair abuttment. "Get out of here kid, the cops are on the way." I stayed, standing watch over the man, until the police arrived. I told them everything I had seen and gave them my name and address, only because I did not feel a part, a party, nor of consequence. I felt as though I was standing in a line, off over there, all alone. I felt like the mental notes I had taken were something I had to dispose of quickly.

Weeks later Roger, that was his name, showed up at my doorstep almost sober. I was too young to be sensibly afraid. In his confused brain I had somehow saved him. As he figured, had I not been there, they would have killed him. So to reward me, he wanted me to come along and watch him even the score at the bar. I said no. He became sullen, wanted a drink and talked in abstractions about himself and his life.

I find myself fleshing out his narrative and adding color. *Because of alcohol he had a criminal record suggesting he was mentally unbalanced which did not allow his enlistment in the marines and a tour in Vietnam, something he craved.*

I alter those facts in my colorizing brain: *he was dishonorably discharged after several incidents in Vietnam. Incidents which illustrated an honorable nature brutally misconstrued by authority and war.*

It was later, when I failed to stop him from raping a woman, that I learned from her that truth, honor and dignity are never absolute and often illusions.

You can be too young to feel the approach of that blood sucking monster, chronic depression. I was falling and had no clue. What saved me is the velcro of creativity.

Shortly after Roger the maniac came my meeting with Max and my immersion in the polemics and dance moves of genuine other bohemia.

1.

Max taught me the four dimensional evidence of a 'working-to-wards,' an absolution only the creative process can serve up. Only in this case the evidence was real. All else was either apology or worthless selfishness.

And the working required for its evidenciary definition structure - form - rules - limits - boundaries - restrictions, any and all of which were absolute and temporary, in service to the creativity required.

The force, the anger, the insistance, the demand of Max came out ahead of the caravan of his life. Intellectual Bohemia was the thing, otherwise why would I have gone there? There was a second-hand, affordable, hand-scrambled quality to the smells, sounds, decorations and rationale of this new/old world, untied as it was from the acceptable normalcy of a Richard Nixoned formica and whiskey society in combat with Vietnam war protestors and dime-store psychedelic theologians. This 'other' bohemia, this decorated intelligentsia, this after-party gypsy-like crystaline rattle-space reached out constantly for fragments of culture to patch together in aesthetic-chewing taut-balance; persian wall hangings as tablecloths, chunks of newspaper headlines stapled to the walls, a cloth glove stuffed with pennies and hung from the toilet tank chain and on that tank the scribbled Wasteland words of T.S. Eliot insisting no context required, a broken chunk of curly-cued wrought iron railing nailed to the pantry door header from which to hang long strands of threaded pasta shells, an Elmer Bischoff slap and dash ink drawing inviting Franz Kline to leave the party, a bust of Walter Pidgeon, a pigeon wearing a mask of Bruno Walter, fourteen tiny toy trucks some missing wheels all glued to the edge of the clawfoot bath tub, the juxtapositon of bits and pieces of garbage - wrappers, bottle tops, moldy bits of hard cheese, tiny braided stand-alone pigtails, single earrings, single shoes, single theater tickets, single doorknobs, and every damn piece of it a perfect ornament. But most important to me, every single thing right where it belonged.

To a young coward it screamed, NOW IS THE TIME to PICK Your CONVEYANCE. (I'm telling this so I can shift now without danger of entering a death spiral. I shall return at a most inopportune time.)

Within this I chose picture-making as my primary boundary set. For decades the modern world has come and gone and come again to the idea of picturemaking. So what? The modern world offers no absolution, no intellectual rest area, it offers only a passing membership in clubs of fashion, taste and market.

"Modern" no longer is. Modern once implied certain inevitability. That fragile balance is gone. Modern has become predictable and as such imitative and banal.

Max put up a notice on the college bulletin board asking for someone to sublet his flat and painting studio. A phone call had established a meeting place on Market Street during the St. Patrick's Day parade. All the world changed in that meeting, it finally shed the shell. Deep dive right into the folds of the oyster.

s.

Violence, class warfare, the hardening of the most vulgar edges of organized religion, comes at us as the expense of the rule by corporate edict and ethic.

t.

Is the cruel observer ugly because of his failings or is it that such destructive asides delay the reckonings? Look at the mess! What does it say? As my father strips himself of all worldly possessions, save security and simple creature comforts, has he discovered something of the definition of worthy existence? Or - is he unwinding himself out of some perceived requirement of exit from this life? Am I ready for him to go? Am I ready for my mother to go? At this late stage of my own life I am not thinking of the great unwind, I am planning and thinking more of the perfect gathering in. What clouds it all is my frequent returns to worthlessness. Is it as if I require some regular emotional correction only available if shown the horrible collapse I seem to promise? Do I require regular bouts of self-induced terror? Where is that macaroni screen now that I need it?

u.

Who are Los Islaños? Those Jews and black Moors of Spanish assimilation who were flung to the Isle of Dogs, The Canary Islands, only to find themselves generations later scattered across the Caribbean and into a dark corner of New Orleans. Los Islaños, purest of mongrels holding on to the promise of earned heredity. Indignant in their belief that Inquisitional fascism's evil would grant them the default of righteous existence. Willed by the first corporate dogs, the Catholic *reprehentia*, to go away, to disappear, to fall off the edge of the world, these offspring of perfect meldings fled knowing a time would come when they would own themselves where they came from, what they smelt like - sounded like - danced like - ate like - smiled like - loved like. They would become a people, with or without herald. Hundreds of years later, their dark rancid beloved corner-ward of New Orleans would be destroyed during a hurricane but not by a hurricane. Rather it would be destroyed once again by the corporate dogs only this time through stupidity, greed, neglect and *evangelical reprehentia*. This time they are not to be chased to the edge of the world. No this time they are to be pushed into the rotting carcass of the new Babylonia. Their smells, sounds, dances, food, smiles and love practises are to be absorbed by the omnivorous many-tongued no-tongued five-toed credit-worthy clean-willed white-hearted load-leveling profitizing boardroom. The boardroom; that toilet of rationales, that wide urinal where castrated men and women stand together pissing away all vestige of a human dignity while voting not to vote, while choosing to anticipate the highest rate of short term return and following it like a crazed male dog follows a bitch in heat. The boardroom where digknity is spelled wtih a K and where Adolf Hitler would have felt completely at home.

The sad sweet song of the death of Los Islaños. You can hear it on the wind if you stand, out of sight, in the swamp. The swamp, that nasty tangle of vine, tree, fungus, stagnant water, reptile hopes and melancholia where storms are absorbed and flung back upon themselves. This time, our time, the swamp is as much human failure as reptile hope. This time it struggles to absorb not only the terrible sadness of the death of Los Islaños but also the death of the mysteries and heatwaves of old New Orleans.

The Army Corp of Engineers, the moronic White House, the vulgarities of political impotency, in every quarter the thieves we prefer to call money-launderers, all of them have murdered our nasty sweet beloved New Orleans. New Orleans was the insatiable groin of America. And she is gone. Never to return as before, never. And the American cultural body is not only castrated by the loss, it is rendered souless.

Our (?) best hope is that this new Babylonia, rather than constructing a suicidal tower to itself, will trigger a cultural and social vortex which in turn will become a vorago - a gulf, a whirlpool, a quagmire or marvellous deep place that sucks or swallows up even rivers, and where nothing can come...

v.

Daedulus, that great pagan artificer - artist hero sees our time as a repository of interesting trash. He sees. That is the important thing.

It is difficult yet necessary to hold to the sacred pursuit of sight. What we see, how we see, why we see and the vagaries of all the interpretations. If there is to be a construct, an intrusive pattern, a rhythm logic, it must all first come from sight. What is vision without sight? Vision gives us the ordinary exhalted and repositioned. Vision would give us what not even Daedulus can see, it gives us our own small ladder.

w.

We come back to the forwarding of worthy memories. We dare to dissect that which most likely we fabricated out of urgency. An urgency to have a right beginning to a life of creativity and huntsmanship.

Back to my digestion of the life of Max.

"Pythagorus, an old tradition holds, used to write his verse in blood on a mirror.
Men looked to its reflection in the moon's hoping thus to make his meaning clearer."
- Jorge Luis Borges

Max saw in my young face a reflective surface upon which he wrote his bloody verse backwards, ala DaVinci, thinking, when he returned to read it, all would strike him as fresh and new. He had no way of knowing I would not wait around. I had places to hide in and roads to grade.

x.

I walked, gathered in by Max and Barbara's enthusiastic discovery of me, to an old back street of industrial San Francisco. Their looks to me and back to each other, syncopated by knowing smiles nearly assured me I would know knowing myself: or at least that I might enjoy joining their temporary feast of me.

Their street, Guy Place, was less than a city block long and belied its alley status by dint of a lived-in width peppered by immigrant cooking smells, tempered garbage and old air. Up three flights of dark staircase dank with excused humanity and apprehension, past what I would learn was "Dinner-jacket Stan's" apartment and beyond to the second floor where temporal light framed the door to Michael Radcliff's residence. Michael was a living poet; living in his poetic state, oblivious of any poetic effort, consumed by a tonal universe which never allowed anecdote to violate emotional veracity.

Third floor was Gimblett's flat. Five rooms in line, a railroad flat. First room Barbara's with significant soiled and torn books, floor to ceiling and in stacks on the floor, the library was tickled by a couple of expansive, splayed and enthusiastic plants and a few art reproductions. I remember a color print of a Theodore Stamos painting, squares of color melting into one another. Next room for sleeping and writings on the wall, pictographs and operating instructions for the physicality of marriage. Bathroom, toilet tank on the ceiling long flushing chain with brass ring and bulging cloth glove, T. S. Elliot scribbled everywhere with obscene caricatures of Richard Nixon. Kitchen/dining room rich with onion and olive oil smells, drying plants hanging from the ceiling, small barrels along the wall filled with dried beans and sundry dry goods. Last a bedroom used as Max's painting studio. The largest 12 x 12 foot space I will ever experience. Bare except for the splatters of paint and a taboret with cans, tubes and brushes. Two windows facing a cement-block lined shaft. On the facing wall, a canvas eight foot wide and six foot high, thick blue oil paint closing down on incised marks, all primaries without the customary predictable limitations. Evidence of a battle being waged against greys.

y.

We struck a deal. I would move in and caretake their flat for the 5 months they would be in New York City. They would then help me to secure the flat above them when it became available. Seventy five dollars a month in 1966, hell of a deal.

z.

Inside of me, a battle of ideas, off my feet and playing with theories, arguing for a shedable skin, a removeable heart, a spiritual wig. Don't hold me to anything, I'm fixing, as reaction and as solidity, to leave myself behind and sashay to private melodies back into my hermetic burrow.

AA.

Knowing naivete and the significance of changeable openings, these may be all there is of me. I read a brilliant phrase or sentence and am propelled to ornate understanding only to find, when I return to the same phrase - same context, that the room I had entered may have never existed. Same is said of musical and visual epiphanies. In words and paint I can only struggle to frame those changeable openings in a moveable outline of knowing naivete.

Is the burden of materialism too often the poisonous blood of sophistication? Should we care? Does asking the question violate the culture?

Intensity of prescription, that is what the dogs of our society would demand of its artists of the moment. That and a tellable story. what escapes most is that the artists of the moment are the illustrators of the moment, the followers, the leaches, the reductive cartoonists - or with some little good fortune - the apologists or choreographers. Odd and ironic that in retrospect, we see the outsider artists - in other words artists outside the moment - as the true harbingers and architects of any future.

It's about accepting separation and reclusiveness in order that the persistent and hideous social demands be denied access to creative

process. Human though we may be, it can never matter what the
"many of other" think of what we have done or will do.

AB.

I should have been with you last night. I'm glad it did not happen. My best efforts never belong to "should haves."

Accept for myself that should there be any need for these words
the paintings have failed. The words would come after as curiousity
or need. If curiousity, a separate life is the thing. If need, throw it
away. "I was there because I made myself do it." Who cares? Not I.

AC.

I make pictures. I paint them. A few make it out into the wider
world. Most linger behind, like bits of cloth hanging from twigs,
to mark the trail back. And the trips back have been important to
balance the insanities, to normalize the man, to keep one foot in
the 'real world.' With age I flirt around blowing up that bridge,
that trail. I think with bleeding thought of the true needs. Always
at risk are those things thought today to be most important: the
painting, the writing, the farming, the family and all the passions. I
risk catapulting myself past all that to the disappearing zone, a place
where effort is no longer coachable and all the trappings of human
existence become detritus.

But once again I pull myself back, carefully, slowly, to the bench
in the cliff and I turn to face what I have done. The wall of the cliff
is etched with silly half images, hieroglyphic and predictable with
artifice. Flourishes here and there announce the presence of a master

draughtsman - and no one cares. No one may care. Facility clouds the emotive, the connective, the resultant. And I see, just once, perhaps for the first time, that such presumptions are necessary placeholders for a reductive culture afraid of its own shadows. Leave the flourishes be, pile them on, fill the canvases with delicious clutter and counterpoint, emblazon the pictures with impossible carnivorous beauty and surpass yourself, always surpass yourself.

Pianos are like that for me. I always feel as though the pianist, not the composer or the orchestra or the quintet or the conductor or the audience - the pianist alone is able to eat himself in his play, devour the coating tone of the notes just passed as his fingers chew - by insistence and measured gathering - the notes just to be now while the eyes of his soul moisten in anticipation of what's yet to come. Eating the meal of music three or four times. Painting is like this for the most fortunate painters. Anguish and self-doubt aside the grateful painter eats himself in his play devouring four times his best efforts.

AD.

There is a shelf between thought, between thinking, between thoughts. A shelf of empty which energizes the purpled spirit by catch and release of the apprehensive nonsense.

"As to pictorial license. It is frequently to this that every master owes his most sublime efforts: the unfinished condition in Rembrandt's work, the exaggeration in Rubens. Mediocre men cannot have such daring; they never get outside themselves. Method cannot govern everything; it leads everybody up to a certain point. How is it that not one of the great artists has tried to destroy that mass of prejudices? They were probably

frightened at the task, and so abandoned the crowd to its silly ideas."
 - Eugene Delacroix

AC

Perhaps context IS everything. Joshua Bell, arguably one of the finest musicians alive today, yesterday went into the Washington D.C. subway with a ball cap and an open fiddle case on the floor. He played Bach while thousands walked past, ignoring him. A handful of people, thinking him a starving fiddle player, dropped $17 in the case. Joshua Bell who, on the concert stage, receives standing ovations for his play: Joshua Bell whose recordings have sold into thousands of homes. In the subway his brilliance was met with indifference. It is no change in comparison to the reception of Cezanne by his neighbors, nor Milton Avery or David Smith to theirs. We, many of us, do not see unless the context proclaims, demands, presents and insists. So much is lost to this curious condition.

AD

Back to the polemics of Bohemia and Maxwell Gimblett. Might have been 1966 or 7, that year of living the smells of hunger and intense creative discovery, that marvelous year of peeling paint and peppered onion ooze, that glorious year of triumphant self-discovery and delicious misery. At night walking the restaurant alleys of San Francisco looking for edible discard. Begging for soup bones, partnering up with Barbara on the purchase of a 100 lb bag of rubbery carrots (.50) and a 50 lb. bag of turning onions. We grated the carrots in her kitchen and, after peeling back the rot, chopped the acceptable portions of onions to mix together in big frying pans as a "hash brown" carrot concoction. It was very fine to an intensely hungry stomach.

Those were the days and nights of internal horizons where the sky of my young soul slid belly first along the rough geology of craggy portent. We were the *center* of the universe and we knew it.

AE

Always able to see (feel) into the future, I knew the terrible extremes; those loves and the losses, those maybes against the nevers, the brush with birth and the hammer of death, the clean white against the rancid mildew, the good exhaustion - the bad exhaustion, the earned pleasures up against the stolen self-inflicted pain. Yes, stolen and self-inflicted both at the same time. It's that background drum beat, ringing in the inner ear of self-annihilating super-imposed inadequacy. It is why I must never quit, for the 'quit' is to let the dogs of failure devour me alive. And though I say never quit, I waste time flirting with the script of predictable disaster. It is as if there is a devil's promise of absolution.

AF

Yesterday it was the loss of 'significance'. This morning it is a leaden weight keeping me pitched towards regret. It's time to use the mind to trim the carburetor of my spirit. The choices are all there, they need no allegory. Go to where the colors form the surges of emotional conveyance and pick the direction with corrective suction. If the platform shell has a dull sandy surface - judge that against your need of hope. If instead it, the shell, is lined in a lustrous pearlescence, sniff out that one and ask yourself, 'will it have a lifting and lasting force?' And remember it's not about you - you, your physical self, it's about the 'us' of you and your passing moment, your passage, your payload, your agreement with the shape-shifting weighmasters of temporal life.

And to 'go where the colors form conveyance' is in actuality to 'record.' Draw, write, paint, think deeply, about what is witnessed and the recording action enlarges the vision. That enlarged vision is the inertia of superb livelihood which, at the everyday pursuits of labor and survival lends the fresh gratitudes which trim the sails of the blessed spirit. Never with an audience. Shield the eyes from any view of those who watch. Insult them with your lack of social discipline, your refusal to acknowledge their needs, your very hopelessness. For why would you want an audience for exercise?

The blood-shot critics hasten to observe that darkness equals depth and complexity - aspects of a definition of worthiness. They look for the chewable and discard all else. They squirm when time proves them inconsequential. They need the general audience to hide their commonness. We critics, we stinking rotten moss-begotten critics. We empty vessels of neediness gone rancid.

AG

I still smell the dark serpentine staircase at Guy Place where the ornate fetid odors of poverty mixed, in bottomless layers, with garlic, pepper, oregano, citrus, toilet leavings, and cheap perfumes. The old cinnamon, tobacco and rosemary smells of the nearby Mc-

Cormick-Shilling factory blended well with the diesel and exhaust fumes of the Bay bridge on-ramp. It was a time when there were a handful of great guitarists, a few magnificent painters (Edward Hopper was only just dead, and Picasso doubly mean-spirited in his last reaches) like Lobdell and Diebenkorn and Avery. It was a time of seperation and reach, top to bottom. The middles were set, far off to the side. Unlike today where the excellent guitarists number in the hundreds of thousands and the magnificent painters are as blades of grass. Was this a goal? A cruel goal? Because the excellent guitarists have become spiritless and common. Because the magnificent painters bleed their colors in the wash of humanity. Now all is middle and muddled to boot.

Or?

The true tops and the true bottoms are by necessity invisible. Weights and measures require yardsticks, standards, accepted units. Just as the Food and Drug Administration does not recognize herbal remedies, our society in its modern guise no longer recognizes excellence of the spirit.

In 1967 the view top to bottom was aided by the funghal aspirations of the crawlers struggling to sight the goals and the abyss. The crawlers as beneficial parasites. The crawlers not the bottom feeders - there is of course an important difference. The bottom-feeders are vision-less cowards, thieves of sweat, cheats, horny cultural voyeurs. Today these plagiarists of human spirit are everywhere and frequently in charge. In '67 they were in hiding. In '67 crawlers found the tops and bottoms and gathered respectfully as though vultures at the rotting carcass. When the jackals and lions of creativity spotted the gatherings and moved in to realign their relevancies, the vultures, the crawlers, stepped back to wait their turn. 'Ah' the grotesque, necessary civility of the interdependent multivores.

But it all started to disintegrate by '68. The new age became the silly age of opaque revelations and emotional cosmetics. Such a narrow, terrible beautiful cusp to roll off of backwards.

AH

Always it had been a race to mature, to get where I was no longer too young. Too young to understand, too young to join in, too young to be in the game. Much later I realized it wasn't maturity I lacked, it was attitude. Not the attitude or attitudes of substantial inquiry and doubt, but rather the pretense that all of it was just no big deal. A young man of volcanic passions and high arching cynicism is assured of being left out.

So when the intense scrutinous gaze of Maxwell Gimblett poured over my eighteen year old sensibility and said, "you look like a young Kandinsky." my mooring set itself to his ankles and for the longest year of my life I was drug in his wake.

When long-fingered Stephen Greenwalt came to visit from my Santa Barbara past, we found ourselves, red wine in hand, at Max's doorstep. We were ushered into the linoleum womb of Barbara's kitchen and seated round the little pock-marked red table. From behind us the linseed oil, tobacco and turpentine odors were excruciatingly magnetic. I either wanted into his studio or into my own. But Steven had come for communion and to argue about the secret scriptures of art. Max, thirty two and worried that he was too old to play peer to these two Rimbauds of shallow footing and long toss, grew angrier with each glass of wine. Staring at us both across the candle light he fingered the fork at his table side and asked, "What of justice? Justice have any place in art or for artists? No goddamit, it bloody well doesn't! You want justice?" He yelled as he bent the fork in front of his face. "I'll show you justice!"

And he threw the fork at me, striking me hard in the chest. "Bastards! Young bastards! Get out of my house, take your young pretty asses and your virility the hell out of here!" And he got up, crying, and locked himself in the adjoining bedroom which served as his studio.

The next day I met Max on the stairs and he acted as though nothing had happened, making soft caressing pleas to see how my crucifix paintings were progressing. No apologies, no recriminations, no set-aside. Forty plus years later it remains one of the large lessons. In those moments I was old enough. I continue to struggle to return to that age, apprehensive that it may come sooner than I am prepared for. Mind stay with me!

AI

Forcing myself to write each day, especially when I have little to say, threatens to disfigure my love of the process. But love of the process may be one of the reasons that the writing itself feels empty on the read. No, that's crap. Love of the process is a good thing. No, my problem comes from the self-analysis. Always probing the fleshy parts of a next move. When the probe falls behind the immediate action, pearls fall from my cranial sack and sing with their bounce. It is very much the same with my painting. When I think and analyse and prepare I seldom create fresh. When the brush stays well ahead of this forward brain, the freshness pours out like those pearls.

Back in 1967 Maxwell showed to me, by example, the terrible intense beauty of the unflinching absorption and critical push. Because of this, I believed for quite some time that the only creative excellence came from a tortured, totally immersed dedication to self-cricitism. It was behavioral and destructive but I would not have traded the experience for anything. It gave me an outer skin, some distance away from my deepest true sensibilities. It gave to me a personal 'or' to a long life's progression of 'either or.' Some of my branches may have been barren for decades but they are still there forming a tableture for notes to be tested upon.

The lessons Max taught me have long since ceased to be of intrinsic value. But the teaching, the branding of my existential hide, the feel of the heat, the nature of the love, the scope of the jealousies, the caustic curiousities remain with me still.

AJ

There are at least two black-haired girls which haunt my past, my youth before youth. They, every one of them, taunted through their melancholy, taunted with their melancholy. In today's time rife with answerless violence and commerced inhumanity, the soft shaping notions of melancholic taunt give valued form to the possibility of re-enchantment.

AK

Who is to know what's worth saying let alone thinking? Talking, writing, thinking, they all need to happen. Silence is loneliness and lonely thoughts seldom leave a trail. I depend on trails. Not so much for seeing where I came from or where I'm going as to pick up pieces of other trails to give me at least the illusion of breadth. I liken it to what happened to my painting. Smart I thought I was when the courage came to abandon the figurative and work solely with abstraction. Until I began to suspect the stylish comfort of unaligned and unapologetic design, and felt myself re-attracted to the figurative which had given me operatic apologies and telling alignments. Then there has been the bonus of discovering the glue of beguilement, something easier and more sincere with the figurative. So, just as it is with words, as a painter my job is to sustain the flow. Too much time before the blank paper or canvas is silence and trail-less loneliness.

AL

Running alongside just past the fringe of brush cover, I have had the most fleeting and limited taste of the society of my own moment. There have been times, spyglass borrowed from my son's grave, when I have bored holes in my view attempting to understand by core sample what the "they" of "we" mean by all the ugly and stupid manifestations of singular greed.

It is exhausting, this cynical wonder. So we look for the humor, she, my future worth, and I. For there is a "woman" aspect to my claims on any posterity. Not speaking to gentleness but rather the florid excess of sentimentality as emotional cosmetic. These give a only chance at re-enchanting wonder. Filagree the humors and play dress-up with creative pursuits. Allow that the most formal forms of the distant and recent past provide glorious container and rationale for the new chase after fullsome humor.

AM

Fast forward. Flash light on the stupid demarcations of the commerce-driven secular culture and small people with big eyes scurry about, trying to hide evidence of their sentimentality. They don't want to be found out. Because they hold on to the ridiculous modernist notion that our world is being ordered and protected by 'sensationally competent' adults, all of them invisible, insensitive, myopic, selfish god fish.

AN

In those early times of my life, when the poverty was a painful adventure, my property was my soul. Protecting my soul back then seems, today, to have been easy work. Today, decades later, my property is my property and my soul is in hiding wounded by the terrors and cautions of cowardice and possessiveness. Would the loss of property, all property, make of me once again an adventuresome soul? Or a dead failure?

To move by assured walk, gloves in hand, from this time to those past times is to ask after the future.

AO

In those early days of my San Francisco every dime was sacred. Walking was my first choice, from Guy Place across Market Street through the heart of the financial district down Columbus past the strip joints into North beach and to the Art Institute. I walked and walked, perfecting the art of avoiding any eye contact with strangers and blending into the shadows. It was a poetry.

Thinking back on those times I have to wonder at the basic flaw in my personality which pushed me out of that time and routine and into the arms of imagined futures. Married as a child to a child? The death of my first born son? The need to complete - education - evolution - family constructs? The need for acceptance?

Those times were wildly exotic and intoxicating causing me to squirm with impatience for my own full membership, something which was never to happen.

AP

Balanced inside of sanity, or, in other words, insanity is a place completely dependent on support systems. If the individual who is inside of sanity supports himself with internal and external balance beams and points, there are governors in place to prevent the destructive runaway. If, however, that individual is dependent on others for emotional stability there will always be a thin thread holding the moments from explosive destruction. It is a self-knowledge issue. Ramble on but always know. Know that dependency is the disease. "In" dependency is the prevention. We are islands, each to his own. While there is goodness in commonality and community, it is the goodness of the "rest station" of the "tag your it" of the "I am loved" - all and each important but only fullsome spread upon individuality and independence.

So it is with this exercise in annihilating biography. The "looking back" and deeply, into the folds and esophogal spasms, for to find why certain things etched into my being while others came as if a fog which disappeared from measuring memory as it lifted. In my leap frog brain the reaches back and the touchstones of today ask of me "have you done the work to preserve the fullest outside access to this identity?" As daughter Juliet insists, "Dad, sign and date the paintings while you can." My hesitation to sign it all comes from several places. I am not done deciding what should die. I have a wavering sense of the value of any of it. I am not ready to be done. I am still trying to connect my past to my present and future. But

I understand the concern. I may not be ready to be done but then
I am not to know when done is. Sign the stuff. Organize the files.
Finish this narrative as far as I am able. And use caution to organize
it all for preservation and access. Otherwise it is an elaborate fart
into the wind.

AQ

The 19th century German historian Alois Riegl believed in the
artistic will or will-to-form. *"He rejected the idea that art was always
moving towards some single, ideal kind of quality."* His *'Kuntstwollen'*
was his indifference to the historical particular, his downgrading of
evolutionary forces, - his disregard for the autonomy of the individual. In his mind there never was nor is a drive to a perfect classical
vision. Riegl's theorum did not exist in my time of the 1960's, not
for me. But the energy to doubt lineal hierarchies as evidence, jus-
tification and *causis* raced out ahead of us all as if a light from a dead
star of expanded possibilities. The "art world" told us, as students,
what was the latest proof of life in an 'ism' and we tested the asser-
tions at our own peril. We were expected to purchase an 'excuse'
from class and the classical through a trunkload of historical logic.
To do otherwise was to invite the wits and half wits of ideological
regurgitation into the reproductive chambers of our self doubt. To
survive 'intacto' meant a hardening of the presumptive shell.

At that early stage and age I took aim at the creation of a varied
and vast body of work of selected reference and no particular avant-
garde homage. My successes have been my own and reside in the
deepest folds of this silly and singular life.

AR

The summer of '65 was adorned by the hesitant attentions of a young woman. She was lovely beyond self-knowledge. A voice so quiet and smooth that it disappeared into the waiting folds of that needy time, she would lay her hand, curled, against my own shovel-grip. She listened, eyes down, to the torrent of grimy ego insistence. Those words, my words, had no 'sharing' to them. It did not matter to her. What mattered was the 'false adhesion.' She needed to be stuck to me and to have me be stuck to her. At eighteen years of life she was old and ready for the devotions of an unselfish adherence to the needs of another. She did not want partnership, she wanted to be taken as chattel. I knew none of this until now. And I know it now because, in Dickensian fashion, I am being made by my own ghost to revisit and understand.

The Next Part

1.

The wall gave no clue it contained a door. Once open, the door
violated the wall, the space it contained, the space beyond and polite
notions of passage. Untimely comes to mind, as in untimely death.
Timely death, however, should lack as much propriety even with the
sauce of sentiment. Of course there are those heavy arguments of
the sanctity of life, insincere by virtue...

It was the Eugenean Bill Wooten who lent me Heidegger's "Poetry, Form and Thought," I suspect because at twenty something I
posed a small threat to society's somnamulism. Without the necessary constraints of form, I was told to expect my natural intellect
would eventually become just one ingredient in the human omelet I
was destined to become. Discipline, as in self restraint, is a movable
enclosure or a delusion. Make the choice before it is made for you.

Choosing to leave the bedrooms of academia and the alleys
of commerce to go for a farming life ended any possible threat to
society. I neutered myself completely and with no remorse. Where I
went I am. Where I am I went. With solitudes and spaciousness un-
available in clusters of men and unacceptable in gaggles of women,
I have learned the arts of self-gagging. Now, in these platinum years,
if permitted, it is time to lob the stink bombs of fetid wasted beauty
into the convulsed marketplace.

2.

Labor is the equalizer. Physical fatigue the evidence and the
reward; for fatigue makes most anxieties almost bearable. The poetic

soul cannot help but infiltrate labor's process with ample if quiet insistance. The Guadalupian designer of effort has nothing on the spirited farmer, on the lotharian gardener, on the insipid choreographer of timbering. Trash, trash, trash; over-reaching trash. But that's the humanity of it. Truth's not here. It's out there, when the long vestments are worn and the salutations forget they are eulogies.

3.

Light flashes bounce off the periphery and remind me of the last moments of storm at sea. Salty greens oil the senses and the light cuts a pattern through which accomplishment seeps, creeps in the outside of fatigue.

4.

Winter of '66 in San Francisco, the moistenings forgave old cardboard, old concrete and the shuttered eyes. Salesmen and creeps used their eyes, angered authority used eyes, the deranged sometimes used eyes. Otherwise survival was about the blending into shadow, survival was in not being seen, survival was "no" to connect, death and destruction were the flag of the smiling open eye. Even so it was an intoxicating time and place as if Brueghal had created a four dimensional cartoon of work, shelter, misery and frozen commonality. 'Neath it all was the suggestion of rich musicality, the long truffled chords of Bill Evans, the shrill calls of Eric Dolphy, the chamber sounds of MJQ, the comedian's sour shorts, the inflated breasts.

For a precocious child of 18 it was a trolley ride deep into the buggered promise of deepest desires and the soul's confusion.

Miserable carpets, the stench evidence of terrible failed lives, perfect beautiful terror of unprotected discovery. Every release, every encounter a menu of possible departures and no backup anywhere.

In those days the concept of hope was foreign and useless. Not to say it was a hopeless time, rather to say it was a time so full of chance that hope could not keep up.

And I devoted myself to painting at a time when the first whispers of this art's end were blowing across the last highball. Coming smack atop the heady excesses of abstract expressionism and dragging forward the comic spastic intrigues of surrealism, some were to be forgiven believing in a future for the painter's passion, but visual poetics were adrift and feminine snobbery coupled with the commerce of synthetic experience worked overtime to mock any who would pursue Delacroix's dream. Sincerety was the first casualty, then gratitude fell.

5.

The Haight district of San Francisco was Russian; staid, moldy, dulled save for the cabbage odors of dough balls vinegared with meat stuffings. Those old cafes were as if temporary invasions of private parlours. Large-boned women, with sad thirsty smiles aproned against invasive sound and value, pushed plates of exotic northern herbaled starches forward past unfortunate apologies. Angry old men, whiskered deep inside, tossed squirts of eye socket venom, anxious to keep youth and naivete in their place. While the very oil of their conservatism, their orthodoxy, made of this neighborhood a magnetic vacuum. As if "leave us be" translated to "we need your invasive foreigness," the first of the post-Kerouac feather-heads oozed in through the cracks to absorb stolen ethnic acids and low-rent victorian hovels. The Russians must have left on rainy nights for no one saw them go. One day they were there, the next it was psyche-delia's picnic ground. From hard old truths to soft young ferment, from Prokoviev to Big Brother and the Holding Company.

6.

On the television news the last breath horrors of South East Asia were served up as the first vulgar reality shows. Bang he's dead, bang the child is dead. The screaming mother - bang your dead and now this word from Chevrolet. Some looked away fearing what this might cause them to do, some could not tear their eyes free, capti-vated by the inescapable truths, thrilled by the destruction, titillated by the abject suffering, altered/drained/devastated by the actual witness of death. And we call ourselves a people? Fortunate for the soul of many a third group, swelling in number, screamed in unison "Stop the war! Stop the war!"

Villains of classical proportions and lasting value papered our collective psyche. Manure-soaked rutabagas riddled with maggots and oozing the rancid oils of darkest greed, their names to become synonymous with stupidity and evil; names like Nixon the para-noid, McNamara the arrogant, Johnson the apologist, Haig the presumptive, and, and, and... Names to join the ranks of Nero, Ca-ligula, Hitler, Amin and company. The club has grown too large to list. And even today we add names. Willy nilly, as humanity screws itself down into the ultimate landfill we call earth. But its all a lot of crap-ass speechifying. True matter of enchanting value only comes of the generous dream, of the thankful appreciative dreamer. All else is acid and emptiness.

7.

The future is always out of reach, it's a place the wind rushes to, it's the backdrop to hollow, it's the cliff edge of uncertainty, it's the moment just past death, it's the wind-torn apple blossom, it's the as yet unfertilized egg, it's the teaching without test, it's the forgotten love.

The bathrooms and latrines of the radical sixties all seemed to pit Richard Nixon against T.S. Eliot. Today loyalty has become a euphemism for demanded complicity. And the bathrooms are free of graffitti.

8.

Do I actually believe these things, this life of the mind? The value of gathered words and paint? The strength of larger quiet thought?

9.

The man, now old, had drunk non-fat milk for so long that the taste of fresh raw milk was odorous, thick front and back, and sweet like a baby's diarrhea. The new non-secular puritanism, the new emotionally thuggish fascist conservatism, the in-grown funghal-brained school-board cowardice of a corporate-ruled journalism; - this sanctioned female society has criminalized a predictable slice of cultural insolvencies from smoking to driving while eating, from eating 'wrong' things to driving without a seatbelt, from disciplining a child to burying a dead horse, from urinating on anything cyber to cooking with real butter. It has driven the old men to revolt. It has driven the young women to act like old men. It has set the stage for re-objectification and for full-on ambulatory life-wrestling wherein the individual human being walks twice as much as he talks and four times as much as he works before a screen. And never walks without purpose.

10.

Back then there was no selecting the wave to be ridden lest that came early on in the selections of day, beach, attitude or posture. As a young man I rode what came and soon after lied about the size of the adventure, not always to obvious advantage. Sometimes I found that lying to make myself out as bumbling fool was to overall advantage. So what the hell was I to do with such girlish contradictions. I hid them, ate them when I could, bent them, folded them, dipped them in coloring molds to give the appearance of great age. I made of my ridiculous anecdotes the walking papers of an ageless charlatan. I extended the measureable boundaries of my life, forward and backwards. Each treasure I instantly understood must be well buried deep within some contextural blankets, otherwise it would fly away on its own, loving itself in a hideous flameout.

11.

The dailies I threw on lawns. Threw them from my cheap bicycle. They were delivered curb-side at our home. A tied bundle which I had to fold into an origamied square I enjoyed flinging onto my customer's yards. The most unpleasant piece of being a paper boy was collecting what was owed. Never easy when fault was dumped on me. And when I felt sorry for someone's inability to pay I just covered it out of my measly pay. Don't remember ever shutting anyone off for lack of funds. Still true today.

The most pleasant part of my job was riding past her house. Most every afternoon I'd see her looking out the big picture window, black hair cut in an Egyptian helmet. Had to be no older than fourteen, chiseled ageless, dark-eyed beauty with the angry-sad look of a spoiled cripple.

She never once looked at me, though I stared enough to fill several stupid cups with longing. My eleven or twelve year old soul wrapped itself, several times, around who she was, how she was, why she held me in my thoughts, how my inadequacies kept the chasm between us lubed and impossible with apology.

Posture was a big thing in my memories of her. She always looked to the left, limp arm drapped over edge of couch back. Head forward, never back. Nefertite neck. Her eyes were the only thing that prevented her mouth from falling off her face. Pull down though it did, her mouth could not free itself from widescreen Fado eyes that sang ahead of and behind this young girl's selfish and beseechless spirit. In my capture I was confused for the first time as to the full peculiar insolvencies of love's debt to the sky-wide mystique of a loverless love. I was in love with love.

12.

Remembering I forget, the rush is to capture each memory and each pivot, trusting the wave to the insistancies of an imagined frustrated reader. You don't understand what I'm trying to say? Here, let me back up and fill in those blanks created by my haste. As long as you hold on to each thread you shouldn't get lost. Also it helps to recognize the onslaught of self-lubricating imaginations.

13.

At the end of my afternoon paper route I would visit a corner soda shop, slash, burger joint. The routine was to drink outside under the shop overhang, near my bike, while, in 1957 to 58 I listened to my jukebox selection, "Rain Drops." Day dreaming about that black-haired girl, no where near understanding how the complex mix of physical and cerebral urgencies were the earliest brewings of a 'manure tea' for my fecund soul; half a century later I come to realize it was all about the life of the mind, all about creativity, all about the passage of such perfect, fruited experience on into something to feel, to say, to write, to paint. All into painting, all into farming. All into setting up spaces that sing and hum with aknowledgements and gratitude. It was never about ownership or belonging or inadequacies or consumation. It was always about pivot.

14.

Now, in the plain and awful dissolve of my disguise I listen, aghast, to brother's discuss the dentist's insistence that ninety three year old father needs to have upper teeth pulled to accomodate a new denture.

To see, no feel, the clearest separation of the lattice-work of his deep resounding memory - fertile with its endless root system - from the skin-thin need for meanness. Not to suggest either indentured to the other, the memory at work is mostly generous save where selfishness is triggered. Is it observation or my own velcro-nature which shows me this relational epilepsy?

15.

Nature's balance shuffles in predation and disaster to hold the mix. Since the inception of the industrial age, man falsely believed he had no predator to fear save other men but such has not been the case. Man created the artificial lives we know as corporations and computers and both have been eating away at the hearts and souls of people for a very long while. Corporations have all but dissolved that saving grace, collective human culpability. Within the next few decades we will no longer be at immediate fault. And computers have eaten away the human mind. Soon "thought" will be a curiousity of the past. Humans are devolving into a vegetable form. The question of the age? Can we put those two, computers and corporations, back in the can?

16.

In 1966 a girl-woman grafted herself to me, and less so I to her. We moved about together not realizing it to be about a last reach back towards a domesticity we never had, fabricating for ourselves a safe zone which never was. Spirits alive to me then warned this was to be my destruction, my fall to normalcy, my final and first flirtation with the haircoat of inevitability. I was they say throwing "it" all away.

17.

Tears have flowed in grotesque volumes without, we know, the slightest effect on humanity's spiraling descent.

Looking back now it is available to me that I might wonder if oily memories of magic time were more that time than my time, my formative time, my hormonal ballet of hovering discovery?

With this memory a frail assistant, I go back on command to that time and its evocations of flutter; aroma passing through forests of darkened wet on into the center of pulsing creamy light. Falling away are those useless concerns for how anything might "appear" to the judges, might "feel" to my parked self. The voyage is a time travel and I become a dipper able to carry forward the unapologetic mosaics of this Persia of hungers, this whistling lizard time, of this elegant slow-roasted impatience, a translucent blanket of changeable relevance. We might become again the Sumerian warrior, the Egyptian mother, the Nubian chief, the Paiute root-puller, the cleaner of ballerina's shoes, the tailor to wizards, the eskimo's least favored child, Vatel's dishwasher. We might hum as we sharpen Villon's pens or wipe Rimbaud's quivering chin. But all of those times are coated in the perfumed stench of the sideways wind of untethered magic.

"Together" as if it be a large or larger matter. "Together?" You want it? What j'u willing to give up? No other way it gonna happen. Got's to give up somethin' And not just any old thing. You have to give up something what defines you. Something that hurts. Don't call it love. Call it giving and giving up. Yep. That's what it is.

She can't want you, not entire. She wants the tethering not the tether or the tethered - just the tethering. Because deep inside she understands that anything less will not deliver her her own desirousness, her own loveredliness, her own spastic self-actualizing 'I knew it all along' self-loving mirrored reading of "the world stops here now at my feet." Doilies be damned.

18.

Sleeping pill in hand, I fight to the death of this old soul for essential humanity. Dreams aligned perfectly with the actual of this nasty time, the separations so clear they stain the widened nostrils; there are techno-zombies in every room who see nothing of the rising tide of uselessness. The old class structures will not hold against the filters of their own insistent sufficiency and strong internal flame of usefulness. And the 'they' will be the man, having succumbed to ever-lower commonalities. But even such observations are sickness as we continually choose the wrong battles. Who is to say that "essential humanity" is a worthy flame or even a flame at all?

The branch breaks. A short fall, a deep breath, a new branch to hold for now. For though the words may fail to hold the waters of truth they nonetheless point towards an energy lit by clarity of purpose and the songs of right livelihood.

The prayer should be: oh give me this day the chores I may do to sustain and create life, to grow the findings of new clear purpose, warmth, charity, and longevity as our natural gratefulness fertilizes futures beyond us. May I always be so fortunate to enjoy the protective embrace of souls larger than my own as I go occasionally to my smaller self. For ours should be the power and the glory of grace as it comes to us from the song of loved purpose and magical beauty manifest.

19

Time of day can alter perception's mood. Morning, after dawn, has always had a moderating effect as if to say here's that next chance you wished for even if you never allowed the words to come out.

My San Francisco Art Institute of 1965 still had the monastic glum and stench of a California mission complex, soaked in fog rather than sunlight. That courtyard fountain centered, roofed foursided, internal porching barely sheltering the high anxieties of student oil paintings ripe with odor and the unapologetic jab and splash surrounding and naming Soutine's influence, the afront to the Diebenkornian academy. New York reined supreme with the Warholian and synthetics wrestling the power dance with Stella and Greenberg's toys. Hopper, Morandi and young lyricists claimed the reaches and continue posthumously to show a way above. It might be observed that 1965 was the last year of an unquestioning supremacy for the true human signatures. Synthetics, synthesis, the plasticizing of plastic theory, the elongation of nihilism and the punjab of lyricism all seemed to gain a strong toehold. Duchamp won the day in ways even he would find distasteful, for the first casualty was context. The abstraction of abstraction, satirizing satire's look upon its own excesses in ways which could only result in odorless renderings of fecal matter as emblematic of synthetic feces assigned to artifical digestive systems.

But, in those classrooms we did not see it coming because of the assignment to learn each medium and ourselves only from within process.

Outside influences were suspect, outside as in "away from" the sphere of the Institute. That couldn't last long as much because of music and theater as anything else. Sopwith Camel, Jefferson Airplane, Big Brother and the Holding Company and The Mystery Trend punctuated the time and place with sweet wails and percussive efforts far above the mediocrities of Leary and company. And those riffs pulled us, compliant or not, into that wider world of suspect flavors.

End of that part

Visiting an End

3-a

Writing as I do with a nasty disrespect of any potential reader, a disrespect which would deny the cheap theater of vulgarity - the vulgar theater of our own scabbie emptiness; I say we are laughable in our attempts to deny death's wrenching pull.

Each doctor, each nurse, each orderly, comes to my bed-ridden dying father and asks "how you feeling?" and he finally spits "I must be dead."

"Why do you say that sir?"

"Because everyone looks at me in this bed, obviously sick, as though they cannot see me and asks 'how you feeling?' Goddamit! It's stupid, obviously I'm feeling bad. Damn it hurts, and you know it, but you still ask your stupid questions!"

So now he quits answering and instead stares at the questioner with a disdainful grimace as if to say "God, spare me from this stupidity." His nature remains intact even when his spirit wanes.

What of vitality? What does it mean in any true living sense? Is it cousin to urgency? Or is it the liar's push towards closing, towards completion, towards culmination? For the young vitality is evidenciary, for the old it is desperation's swim suit.

Things to do, get them done. Not for others, not just for the doing, for the done. It is the reward of a long life of doing: now we find we must get more done. Consequence of less importance. Acknowledgement be damned.

Vitality: evidence of the energies 'neath life with or without. Vitality: the bounce enhanced by how a body accepts or rejects that outside world - that conclusive intrusive holdme, slapme, divorceme, denyme, lietome, laughatme, cutme, kissme, colormy-world outside.

It was 1970 and the neighbor came across the highway, panicked by the horror, to plead for help. Her horse had been found standing shakily over a steel post. It looks as though, playing or fighting with another, this lovely young mare had reared up and come down, full force - full weight, upon a steel fence post. Skewering herself in the fleshy chest, just ahead of her left foreleg. She had not been able to free herself, only to fight and aggravate the bleeding. The look in her eyes, and a finger to her gums, said she was in shock.

It was a Sunday and no veterinarian could be reached. I phoned my Cherokee friend and described the situation. He asked,

"How deep does the wound seem?"

"Seven inches or so."

"Cut loose the fence wires and bend the post as you walk the mare forward. Do not let her back up!"

"I'm not sure I can do that."

"If you don't she will die. After you have her off the post flush the wound out with a hose, careful to have your hands clean, peel a banana and stuff it up into the hole. Put lots of tape over the hole so the banana stays in. That should keep her until a vet comes. I think you should go to the vet's house and make a fuss, tell him the mare's gonna die and that I said he was a chicken shit."

When the vet finally arrived I told him what I did. His eyes went wild and then narrowed, "Jerry tell you to do this?"

The mare was saved and later the veterinarian explained how the banana was clean in its skin. Flushing the hole and stuffing the banana up there had held the wound gently open, allowing it to close slow as the banana lost its shape and bulk. He grudingly admitted the genius of the plan but quickly added that Jerry was an asshole - effective and smart, but an asshole none-the-less.

But most stories require an atmosphere of vitality. They don't serve endings so well, they serve middles, the middles we must hold connected if we are to always be of living, always be of use to the demands of vitality.

And to prove the thread-thin craziness of God's chance rhythms, we learn that the variety of banana most eat and know, the Cavendish, is a chance hybrid, a sterile accident of nature. The thing which lends it long shelf life and bruise resistance is the mutative nature which makes it succumb so easily to "Tropical Race Four," that nasty kill-all disease of the banana.

Ironic then that this giant fruit-bearing herb would, in its mutated state, offer a seemingly natural solution to the horse's wound.

For my 94 year-old father there is only one such 'natural' solution(?) to the severe aggravations of pain and physical decay and that is for him to pull his own plug, for him to shut himself down and hope for comfort. He is only awake now for a couple of hours, spred over three meal-oriented slots. And during those times it is apparent his spirit - his vitality is half here, half gone.

He is my seed. He was the man in my childhood for only a long dozen years. He was my mother's enabler. He was an outsized hero

to measure up to. But perhaps most telling, he was my most important adversary, the one whose insistence and demands - all through
life - begged to be ignored.

From the age of 58, when hospitalized with blood clots, he
decided his life was over, though it would not be for nearly 4 more
decades. Bad actor in that way. Hard adversary.

He's gone now, my father. I prefer to think of him still with me.
I prefer to think I will win him over yet. He envied me, a twisted
envy. I wished for his approval, yet somehow we never completely
met. He needed to knock me down. An odd math to this good/bad
relationship.

His last lesson for me is of that curse, to be old and so utterly
purely yourself. All the polish gone, the grain pronounced.

3 - b

I return after a couple of years to this writing and find sketches
that argue with the fiction of the thing. Working from "recent-cy"
it is difficult to maintain that this is not autobiographical - certainly
not ... yet.

Reaching back to the mutated stories of youth, fiction is the aid-
ing salve. Speaking from today, truth is the unarmed and disarming
foolishness... somewhere between the two rests sentiment waiting to
disrail the purposeful.

At this late date to have handed to me by Paul the writings of
Fernando Pessoa is to fill a fractious glimpse of a parallel universe
- loftier, wiser, yet far more sedentary. Each thought cupped and
forced to play within itself for eternity - and in that a wide and fine
applicability. It is as though Camus had a great uncle who successfully hid his philosohical musings from family and friends, thereby

allowing a wallow in the new beauties of self pity.

And in all of that a return to the easy lesson of the cumulative. To pen a few words each day, to make a deposit in this account, is to invite a compounding of reflection, to entice enticements, to feel the undeniable slow crawl to the substantive. It is as if to say that sticking with it will result in an entire new 'complete'. But also to say that 'sticking with it' IS an entire new complete. 'Neath it all are the references for how words as trail of thought do flutter us along.

Sometimes best intentions amount to an emptying.

3. c

In those last two years of my father's life he surrounded himself with boxes of snapshots, photos of his nine decades plus. Fingering through these messy piles, he'd happen on a picture that would set his memoried mind racing in search of a connection he previously missed. He started to imagine motives and possible alternative endings. "Why did your mother choose me?" And that would push him back further, out of her view, out of their meeting on that beach in Puerto Rico. Push him back to the very moment when an ad in a magazine stopped him cold, in darkest Wisconsin, and pinched his view towards the perfumed lit dream of California.

The ad showed a cartoon line-drawing and asked "would you like a career as an artist in sunny California?" He, but nineteen years old, fingers familiar with a deft brush and etching blade, eye married to the absolute truth of the insides of what is seen; he bought a ticket for a bus ride to complete uncertainty. Burbank and the naugahyde promises. Burbank and the rotting orange of monied truths, guerilla economics, and endless tradeoffs. Bungaloed.

The trek a forgotten blur, he entered a lobby, men in lines aimed at a long table. He signed in and was handed a tablet of paper and a pencil. "On each page draw a ball descending, bouncing up and falling again to repeat the motion. We want to be able to flip the pages and see the ball bounce."

Each man went to his station and worked on the assignment. My father sat quietly for a moment and noticed the tall dark moustachioed man standing in the corner nodding his way. He took the sign to mean everything rested on the outcome of this exercise.

He drew a ball carefully, added stitching as though of a soft ball and chose the direction of the light to guide the shading.

Once done with this first page, he carefully sketched the ball, having now dropped slightly and turning slowly, shading and detailing this one as well. Each page, infinite care. And as he finished each page, peripherally he noticed yet another man turn in his notebook and leave. Four hours later, he, the last man in the room, took his completed project to the front table. Flipping through the notebook the moustachioed man nodded and then shook his head 'no'.

"Ralph is it? My name is Walt Disney. You've done an exquisite rendition of a bouncing ball but it won't do. You see, we need men who will draw quickly and simply."

That was it. Three thousand miles to be told he was entirely too good. He stumbled outside into the afternoon heat and blinding light and walked between two parked cars to cross the street. The long, shiny roadster glanced off him at slow speed, knocking him into a hydrant. The driver stopped, rushed to his side and apologized profusely. "Hey, buddy I have to run to an appointment. Take my card. If you're injured I want to know. Get in touch with me, if I can help you." The man was William Powell, the actor.

That chance meeting resulted in my father procuring a job as a body guard for a movie producer. The man was wrapping up production of the movie "The Rains Came" with Tyrone Power and Myrna Loy. Young, strong, bright and insanely naive, my father swam around in the soup of Hollywood with nary a clue of its permanent ink status on society. The man he protected was Darryl Zanuck.

4. a

And in this time, 2012, fully amidst the demands of a pervasive, viral, artificial intelligence, marketed and spoon-fed as the first stages of humanity's final obscurity - we pull at words as though they are rotting teeth with less and less promise for artistic record.

4. b

So to revisit the terrible insides of those storms that would have ended us - had we let them; how are they different from today's today?

When the fabric of society seemed a coursing of many defined efforts and concerns, racing interwoven and side-by-side, fighting back and forth, when it appeared there was cognitive movement; we were lifted and held by an unspoken sense that man's world would find purpose. But today, in the endless search for the new deadening, in the embrace of frivolity and false innocense, we go towards emptied depths, we go aimlessly towards a great final worthlessness... unless...

But what has that to do with the individual triumphs over killer storms? Great sadness, enormous personal failings, horrid endings, loss, and more all piling on till there's a black fog over all next steps.

4. c

We've entered into an age of deadly confusions. A fracturing of the collective human experience into a frightening kaleidescope of explosive force which has destroyed the gravitational pull of the individual soul, the stabilization factors all nearly gone now. There is the risk that this will render the greatest acheivements of man to so much dust. What is to be done? Are we to redouble efforts to keep our creativity close-in, to hold to the old adventures of the written word, the painted and drawn image, the songs, the dances, the structured theatrics? And what of the old ways of living magic? The farmings, the healings, the spiritual inquiries? What of the stories which re-place us into the true adventures of life inside of life?

Somewhere there is a hen-scratched document underway at this moment with the power to return a man or woman to a clarified center of a loved life grounded in understood purpose and dedication.

4. d

I drew water into a glass, prepared, if this fountain pen should once gain plug and require the tip be dipped to free its flow, and found that ink was waiting to release itself. My life is susceptible now to the "indications." The ink flowed freely for the first four lines then seemed to dry up, though this is a cartridge pen. So a dip in the water released ink - now it stiffens once again - and I dip once again...

I have come to a window on madness - or - to the porch of ultimate balance. Known only to me, I am and have been preparing myself so that whatever happens next, barring the death and destruction of others, whatever the outcome or transition might be, it is what I wish for myself. That is not to say I have no over-riding desires or compunctions - it is to say that an awareness exists of under-tows and waves which have the power to carry me away and it is my "job" to ride it out.

The pains in my hands and arms are now the rule rather than the exception. The relief comes only when I allow the weight of each arm to hang freely (or lay loose as I rest on my back with pillow under neck). There is a pinched nerve somewhere at the base of the neck that, through pain and deadening, robs me of my comfort with any simple hand movement. Writing, drawing, painting, have all been affected by this pain. And added to the pain sensation is the loss of any reliable strength.

But enough of this. I need something else to think about, to talk about.

4. e

Let's return the narrative to my father's Mesopotamian time in the California of the Eucalyptus-wrapped banana, the private loquat and the momentary shine.

As bodyguard to a movie moghul, he came and went freely through the oddest of interiors. He recounted to me of the time at a party when he watched the unveiling of a gold-statuette and a discussion of the evolving plan for an annual awards for cinema. The actress Betty Davis was esconched on a couch and listened to the conversation of what to call the award - what to call the statuette.

With a flick of her long cigarette holder she threw off "Oh, that's just a f...ing Oscar!" in reference to her current lover.

The rest they say ...

4. f

That's what I was, 4F. Tried as a teenager to enlist in the marines, follow my father's path, but they wouldn't have me because of my medical history. Instead I became a mercenary artist selling my stuff to anyone or thing that would have me and the pickings were thin.

The social contracts are changing perhaps forever. Time was when "sticking" with a life program was to result in a cumulative worth and value. Not so anymore, flexibility would seem to be the guiding precept today.

4. g

So I went kicking and screaming late by a dozen years, into the twenty-first century, in a leaky boat - fortunately I am in a shallow back-water, well away from the deep sea - but the current will eventually carry me out there. This time no life guard.

5 one part

Those early years sloshed back and forth - from the lower depths to a vanilla decency with linear progression. Inside the poverty of others I became their desperation, inside the easy normalcies I was easy and normal. Whenever I permitted myself the direction of my solitudes, the constructs were often magnificently bohemian - and, in that, comforting. It was the evidence of a mix of imaginings, vision and courageous inquiry, florid in its presentations, an open invitation. The vanilla, though occasionally peaceful, never offered membership in arabesque nestings, never offered tomorrows. The bohemian is a wild gardening of the soul, quick to embrace the patterning of small enthusiasms and larger desires. The vanilla decency was and is all antiseptic, all hospital, all natureless.

Sixteen years old, unawares that it had been my precociousness which won me an important distinction; a one-on-one drawing class with a "master" at the Santa Barbara Museum of Art. He allowed me to be me, in control of a pencil. To this day - half a century later - I feel the power of that allowance. But back then it was a silly side step in a mostly uncertain progression. With music, dance and theater all asking for my involvement and promising me golden futures, I ultimately chose that easiest of pursuits, painting. For each and every time, it levitated my being and gave me glimpses of my own individuality, my own potential worth.

He was an attractive man of attractive pursuits. Candied and empty. To his credit, he fought it all the way and with some significant success. Late he discovered that the only constant in his life was his life. And that was sloppy because he looked always elsewheres for the constant. He missed his own-ness. When we were alive did we know us or want to? Those times we set the pot to boil, did we know ourselves? And what of any of it in this time of assassins?

He frequently awoke midst dreams of people he did not like, people who tore at him because they did not like him. When those dreams annotated real moments of obstruction, he fought back. All any of it meant was that his life pulsed out ahead as well as behind - and that the individual beats wanted to be swallowed by the larger rhythm. And that larger rhythm asked to be orchestrated, asked to be about ornamental gratitude, asked to be singularly alive.

There was each morning. That, in and of itself, a ritual of offered opening, or regard, of tonalities carried forward into the broadsheet of the day. Let us cup the early moments and blow gently on them our gratitude.

He was an old soul in that tormented young shell - buffeted by chemistry and unreasonable longing. He knew to stand a certain way and to keep a heavy foot on his unearned giddiness. Those slow times and echoed doowop songs suited him long before they became diluted and sugared by memory. Thirteen years old with cigarette pack rolled up into short sleeves, and a banana-long gravity knife in jean's pocket, he was a permanently untested cultural hand-grenade. A delinquent's delinquent. Someone who was charged and found guilty of crimes he never even formulated and all just because he looked the part. He was a cross between Sal Mimeo and Nicholas Cage with the brain of Rimbaud and the moveable philosophical hygiene of Fernando Pessoa. He hated the snobs of the upper classes as much as he loved every vestige of spiritual and mental excellence he found in the lower depths of humanity. He was an emotional ka-mikaze, willing to sacrifice how people saw him to the higher cause of how people felt him - how they might remember him. He was incendiary.

And he had no plan to survive, so he blew out the stops. Forgave no one because there was not the time for such nonsense. Every step of the way, he was done before the end. He wore his linguini like a pasta. He hid the knowledge that new plans were pushing old ones off the list and into the refuse pit. This would inform and excuse his ways of departure and termination. From that early age, change meant kicking everything out, kicking loose, and moving on as quickly as possible.

5 another part

When we look for depth, are we looking down or out and away? Are we looking for complete take-it-or-leave it description or powerful suggestion? Are we looking for Borges or Dickens? Are we looking for Durrell or Peter Carey? Are we looking for textbooks or Steinbeck? Are we looking for money or honey? Are we hoping for answers or better questions? Are we looking for love or restraint? Are we looking for leadership, or an antidote to compromise? Are we looking to feel the way we once did, or discover something altogether new? Are we pulling back the dust and heat to see Baghdad Cafe for what it really is? Or are we hoping to find an Airstream trailer full of Bohemian decoration and herbal transgressions? Do we hope that as yet unseen children will bring us the spinning kaleidescope of promise or are we thinking that there ought to be a perfect Reuben sandwich in there somewhere? Do we secretly hope that the best written inquiries never find their way to computer blogs? Do we want the mysterious book to find us?

6.

Heavy, low-set, all of it thick. The browned house hovered beneath a family of Eucalytus trees center of an old citrus grove. Turpentines blended with flavored acids and released in fine sprays to dizzy the heat. Dirt to kick. Porch shade as unfriendly, as a cloak for unimagined low-grade horrors. Sunlight bright enough to change the shapes of what is almost seen.

All of it the moment when desire-born exploded forward into a lifetime of devastation and creativity. A lifetime where self-discovery was always the flip side, ever away, ever simple, ever almost borrowed.

That hot young citrus day just outside the oppressive house, from the deepest recesses of its shadowed porch, that dark-eyed, dark-haired girl of three hundred years inhaled the boy and spit him out. His shell too tough, she sucked him out the soft backside, chewed him just twice and belched him forward through rooms of time. Merciless.

She was his first second witch, hers his first second curse. It echoed in his futures, her admonition that he would never amount to anything. Implied that the curse go on to say "without me." A Gothic epic, the ending writ at the beginning. A Gormenghast of cruelest inversion.

So for sixty years plus he walks away from each of the many witches who would own him. His private joke that they would never know his antidote formula for their curses, for their divinations. The antidote was in the overlaps. That each new and old curse pulled the plug on the others - and that the complexities made of all of it a large stained cloth invisible to the single dimension masses. The repetitions and urgencies pushed to that ultimate resolution when he would discover he needed no one because there was no one worthy of his need. In that moment, he cancelled all his overlapping curses and became a watcher waiting for new shape and purpose to find him. He understood the importance of the shell. He felt the security of new forms of anonymity and spiced irrelevance.

He sat at the table and watched seven witches battle for his obligation, saw they were nothing and felt the poisons flow through him for the first time without adherence. He saw the strength in embracing his very own and great stupidity. He became transparent as in never quite here, never understandable, never approachable, emotionally vapid, existentially bouyant.

7.
Empty.

Testing Attendance

A.

Sixty five years, fifty plus of those painting, and I've never allowed as I could write in same space and time. Figured all concen-
tration belonged to painting. Why? Don't know. Perhaps because
the scales of the endeavors are so different. The writing is typically
tight, internal work while the painting pulls body out for the wider
self. Also painting begs those pauses to see where the image is at,
to re-measure all those arrogant notions of control. Writing while
painting, though, wrecks havoc with penmanship. Paradox, the
hand to eye coordination of painting fractures the subtler controls
for pen in hand.

It's all new and that is grand. Widening the on-ramp for the late
life stages which need all the help they can get. No rules.

B.

Ran away from home at thirteen. Hitchiked in a southerly
direction intent on finding a young girl I had met that summer on a
Mexican beach. Took all day to go ninety miles to the town of Paris,
California. Told some convincing lies to helpful drivers. Realize
now that I was lucky to survive that trip. Her family took me in and
made secretive calls to find where I'd come from. (They were intel-

ligently responsible and knew pretending helped the tangled ball of twine free itself.)

It had been the result of three things: the thirteenth year, in some lives, opens in the brain to say "hey, this is my life and I think I've got it figured out." It's that time of flowering when hormones and brain cells compete for color and light and purpose.

The second thing was my destructive relationship with my bizarre and vindictive mother whose hatred of me had amplified as and because I acted out my new powers of thought and feeling. For a lifetime and beyond I have blamed her for the weakness, nastiness and deceit that is my character, but in truth all of that came because I was never shown that character was, in large part, mine to mold. So I "became" as much out of absence as any presence.

The third thing which worked to grant me deliberate flight was the romantic connection. The most defining of externals.

The conventional wisdom would have it that serious writing must come from protected time and space. That interuption is death to the carriage of thoughts to the page. That getting the front brain out of the way is a guarantee of nonsense. The opposite resides and presides - the true stream of consciousness would save us from the sickly sweet predictability of show-tune writing. Henry Miller went for angry sex and found the inside of the universal math of human flux, the uncertain thick edge of the fluttering wind-blown skirt of failed romance.

If it be true that we never paint fast enough, regardless of the rigors of context, then how might that suggestion apply to writing? We never write fast enough, we hold for the right *write* moment when it seldom comes prescribed. If we truly write as we think, or better yet, ahead of our thinking we have chances to be in a flux and of the barking response. There just might be something useful and provocative in all of that. At least the blame goes well ahead, towards what we might have been.

My arms and hands hurt and I am forced to hold this odd thin pen in a gentle pinch. It alters me and my words.

With the passage of time and a regime of magnesium supplements my hands and arms are righting themselves slowly. It helps that this new heavy fountain pen gives added comfort. So back I go to that question - do we write or paint fast enough? Why does the memory of my 13 year old adventure keep bringing me back to this question? Was it the impulse I felt back then - an impulse that took me out of myself?

We often sense or see odd pieces of evidence, difficult to explain or reference - so we dismiss these. Example: when I travel great distances north or south, five hundred to a thousand miles, it doesn't happen but when I travel east or west my fingernails grow twice to three times faster. What possible explanation could there be?

Why do we insist on being told? Told, when the evidence proves contrary? We remember back to those gnarled times with a plan to make them explain ourselves, and it insists itself forward to unexpected definition.

C.

So once again the night terrors return, only now I am somewhat behind them - an observer tied to the fight. Unsure, as always of the outcome, I am most willing to return to the musings of this life transected, if only as momentary escape from the horrible evidence of the harms I have caused people I love.

That Baja California vacation was early view of the fickel natures of intertwined narratives especially for a mind willing to ask how others on the periphery might remember the same moments. It was 1960, seven of us in the family drove down in our '55 Buick to a cousin's beach house. Whatever the reason I was told I had to sleep on the roof, away from everyone else. I remember a flat-topped building with vegetables and herbs growing on the sandy cap of this large rough structure. It was surrounded by grass-capped sand dunes except for the beachfront. I remember smells, the surf sounds, and a blanket of stars so close I was sure some had snuck into my clothing. Though I was being punished, yet again, and separated - I felt blessed to spend those few nights like a bony swizzel stick in a fabulous sensorial cocktail.

Our cousins were Hispanic with no English. I was forbidden from 5 years on, to speak Spanish. As Spanish was my first language, the immersion in rolling, folded, red-peppered, chocolate word sounds was like a blanket. I was jealous to witness the happy comfort of my mother as she lobbed Castillian phrases into the waiting air of that short visit, jealous that we never saw that "belonging" comfort in our own home.

Walking on the beach I was fascinated to watch saddle horses being ridden in the surf's shallow back wash. Must have been obvious because a tall cinnamon brown gelding approached me with what looked like a ten year old boy on his back.

After we figured out we had to speak English for my enjoined understanding, he asked if I wanted to ride. He said he would let me ride his horse for a quarter. I told him I didn't know how. With innocense instead of courage I slid up on the bare back of the tall horse. A rope came round the neck and withers to fasten and tie to

either side of a braided cord halter. No bit, no hackamore, just a
halter. The boy explained by motions how to pull the horse's head
in the direction you wanted to turn. He slapped the animal's rump
and we walked off along the edge of the receding surf. I looked
over my shoulder and the boy was gone. Didn't matter. The comfort
I felt was real, comfort not security. The horse ambled for a while,
each step pushing water from the sand on the down stroke and
sucking it into the new cavity on the up. Without pause he then
entered a bouncing trot. Feeling like a baby on a bony uncle's knee,
I gripped mane and rope. He made a slow wide arch and trotted
away from the ocean and towards the dunes. Then he broke into a
long lope. Now I was frightened. I leaned forward, head to one side,
and hugged his neck in an effort to stay on. We hit the grassy cap of
a dune and he dug in and lept forward. We were airborn for a very
long two seconds and as I looked down I saw two naked terrified
adults - one man and one woman - shielding their heads from flying
sand as they looked up at the under belly of some great beast - its
form distorted by the sun directly above.

We landed hard yet he still picked up speed - then slowed as we
approached buildings. There at the open gate stood the little Mexican boy, flipping my/his quarter and whistling for my borrowed
charger, my Bucephelus, my first horse.

Story so good I steal it from myself over and over again with
hopes that it become remembered sound.

D.

We have a floor lamp in our house which has something loose
in its electric cord. Our old house has spring in the floor boards.
Occasionally a midnight visit to the toilet will cause just enough un-

settling that the cord jiggles and sets itself up to connect the "juice." When one of the cats or dogs walk by, unbeknownest to us sleeping, the light will come on.

E.

They say "how are you?" They don't ask it. And you ask "I'm fine." You don't answer - you ask. And the up-side-down entryway has a reverse polarity that prevents connection. Unless of course the "statements" are or become pleading - in which case instantly the cursives of the souls entertwine, hold their footings and begin to crawl up the invisible spirit walls.

Hadn't we ought to elevate and amplify our pleadings, if we want to save each other?

F.

One foot larger, one arm longer, an ill-used finger twisted, the head permently tilted, all evidence of the journey and the pattern, established for what may remain forward.

So I talk and write to record past past. For today is my present past as tomorrow will be my future past. Denying, in this way, that time is the perogative of that artist locked within the constant pursuit. We mean it.

The alleys of Santa Barbara, California, ran from hillside, clear through the downtown, up into the Art Museum, and out into the patient Pacific Ocean. It was the early sixties and no one cared about the future. The present was entirely too demanding. Assasinations, the Vietnam War, corporate incest, civil rights demonstrations and the Vonnegut prism all worked together to keep western society in a long toilet time.

A teenager in that time tempered by the perfumed insolvency of Southern California and tested by repeated viewing of televised death, there was no where to go but tight around the eyes and soul.

G.

I had successfully run away from home. Was, I naively thought, ensconced as a welcome guest of the girl's family. She and I had only a chance encounter in Baja but I had blown air into that: blown air until the baloon burst. I now sat believing my own fabrications.

I was surprised to see the Buick come up the drive. When my father and mother arrived, he said nothing, she said "how could you" she left no air for a question mark; she who had beat me, screamed and frightened me, until I had to leave. On the edge of that unwanted meeting, four adults swollen with embarrassement, I did not understand it was about me.

He drove home, in silence - it was hard to believe he was even there. She spit words out over her shoulder, abusing her beautiful accent.

"You ungrateful stupid boy."

Paused for three breaths.

"Ave Maria, how could you frighten your father that way? Don't you know he loves you? I don't know why. You are a worthless Jibarro. We should have left you there. Do you realize how embarassing this is for us. We had whole police department searching for you for 3 days. You are delinquent. You will never amount to anything...!"

We went straight to the Fullerton police station where I was subjected to a ridiculous charade of threatened jail time, all meant to scare me into submission; submission to my mother.

Nothing was ever the same after that. My life was held hostage by the failure of my escape. I was a loss to myself, always prepared to quit, always traveling scared.

H.

At the beginning of this my old age, I sit dizzy in attempts to re-find my agilities of mind and body. I know today that simple record-keeping of the curious trail of life experiences might bring me to myself. I write these three sentences and my hand begins to seize up. But that mustn't stop me.

Black-haired Charlene Robinson was thrilled to discover that I, also thirteen, had run away and been brought back to the police station. For her this was a suggestion that my awkward body held a dark and independent soul which refused the shackles of home and society. For her I was someone who offered escape and nasty possibilities. Yet I never seemed to measure up to the suspicions.

There was that once, when the nervous man approached me at school and asked if I wanted to buy a car. I laughed, said I was a kid and that I only had twenty-five dollars to my name. He took it and gave me the keys to a 1950 Hudson Hornet, showing me the controls and how easy it was to operate the automatic transmission.

Adjoining the school was a partially harvested cornfield, the center already cut out. I took the car there and found myself driving around in a long circle, laughing until two police cars blocked either end. The car had been stolen. This I learned at the police station.

Charlene Robinson was thrilled to see me carted off to the precinct. But it was short-lived. She came to understand me as a passenger of life, not a driver. And so for me the very old fourteen year old Charlene Robinson disappeared except as a memory. She, as much as anything, set me on a course insisting that my life actually happen.

Thirteen and already smoking, hair greased, pushed up, opposing waves meeting in a trough which kicked loose dark brown 'fishing poles' of hair pointing across my forehead to two dark brown eyes each of which lied every day of their lives about what they saw, what they took in, what they cared about.

Every ounce of my creative, inquiring energy poured in those early years into being a sociopathic genius, a wizard of young desire and desirability, a pet hospital janitor for the vapid and lonely. It is at this old age that I set out in many projects to be, or become, the "old gringo" and to deny the shameful truth of a life spent as human placebo. Thirteen years old with sights set on sixty. Always too young and too stupid, but inside deep was the insistence that I owned wisdom, owned vision, that I was headed somewhere powerful, grand and undeniable.

In every black-haired girl I saw the repeating harangue of too young, too stupid, too sneaky, too lazy, too horrid. Always to the side was the need to make the black-haired girls love me so that I might leave them, leave them cruely and with cruelty. To this day I have never succeeded, never felt the retribution I desired, never felt whole in that regard.

When I went to the classroom it was with a racing heart knowing I would see Charlene once again. Starched white blouse, collar up, black fake-leather jacket, tight jeans, small pointy black shoes, her hair black as coal, mid-length and combed as though a characateur of every tough guy in the school. Black eye-liner thick like a felt-tip marker trail. Pretty nose. Eyes screwed in tight with indigna-tion. And a piece of light chain in her left hand.

I remember one day going to class and being nauseous because she wasn't there. Excused, I went to the boy's room and caught a glimpse of her silouette behind the building. She was smoking a cigarette. I watched. She saw me and didn't see me. The string never existed, but it broke anyway.

I.

Fourteen and having been "thrown over" by Charlene Robin-son, I found my own brand of mean. The cigarettes and rolled shirt sleeves (shirt cuffs we called them) added ornament to a desparate need to show life as over-sold. So when I was introduced to my first gravity knife it was clear James Dean and Sal Mineo came from some place that I understood. The knife always threatened to cut me, every time I swiveled its twin barrels to release the blade in a flashing arc.

Nobody was tougher than I was. Except Richard Neese.

I wanted to say "you have no right to talk to me that way." but there was no opening, no opening because he hadn't said anything.

Richard Neese was the coolest cat I've ever known. Had a "gang" when "gang" meant a gaggle of obedient servants hungry for his approval. Richard was so completely in tune with himself it was as if he were sitting in on a replay - aware at every turn of what would happen next. Yet he was also hungry to discover new currencies. That's where I came in.

He'd have me draw taboo subjects like topless girls driving hot rods. Then he'd dole the pictures out to his gang as rewards for their obedience. My reward was to sit unquestioned at the right hand

of this overlord. It was a lesson in colonies and colonization, it was
an intro into the thermal dynamics of crowd placement. It was the
Little Rascals meet Carlos Fuentes in a Beckett play about the birth
and death of cool. It was a long intense time lived in a plywood
clubhouse with urine-soaked furniture and cigarette-flavored jokes.
It only lasted part of a summer.

J.

Pitchforks in the sand. That until a pause made it clear it didn't
work. Then an over-the-shoulder thought of suitable tools. Writing
can be that way. What interests me more is the discovery that the
pitchfork did not fail, we did because we did not allow that the tool
changed the job.

K.

For the artist in me it's always been the need to clear some space
for the new work. Push that junk in the corner, sweep the dirt under
the rug. Leave off with the 'necessary' paperwork. Just create. No
intelligent maintenance or preparations. Just paint just write.

Years of that and the confusing piles get thick and high. The
loose ends become old spider webs. Accurate memories become few.
The flux in all of it works to ooze together the visible fragments to
complete the legend that heads towards a usuable disposable myth.
Played up or played down. Its all still real to me, still real _of_ me.

L.

Far to the rear of the home property was an old travel trailer, nondescript and yet iconic as a foil-layered bulbous form with one round black tire on each side. The door made tentative noises. The step was hanging and bent. Inside, on the collapsible table, were my oil paints, a canvas panel, and a still-life made up of a glass pitcher, old lace, brass cup and a pocket watch. On the rumbled bed were a handful of cheap, small, art books the pictures of which were faded and stupid in their presentations. This is where I lived and worked as a teenager, with limited security from my mother. She never came out there always disgusted, always afraid, always superior. She never understood and never will, her black hair a crown of indifference.

Can there ever be a time of release? Perhaps not extended. But in many of my time slots, painting in that little trailer, I was flying in a magnificent zone of freedom and purpose.

My father had given me the simple, plain key to it all. He had said, repeatedly, "you have to look hard at what you wish to draw, never 'think' you know what's there. 'See' it even if it doesn't look right to you. 'See' it and then let it flow through you to your hand."

After a long life with many side passes, nothing else has fit for me. And my first rock solid experiences, brush in hand, in that trailer, have joined with all the other such into a river of creativity which has given me rest, exhiliration and purpose.

It was the fourth grade and I had an assignment to write a report on Simone Bolivar, the South American leader and general. Don't know where it came from but the idea presented itself that I draw and paint an image on the front of the report folder of an elaborate native of Bolivia. I am guessing now that my father offered small specific assistance. What I do remember is how with poster colors I watched for days as the image grew right off my finger tips - grew to intricacy and power. There were no acceptable words then to explain it, but I know, myself, that I was showing to myself my self. I was being born into the work clothes of a painter.

That first painting of the Bolivian chieftain was the talisman. I allowed it to brand me deep inside as I went in search of indications of what I was to be. I had become, at that silly age, what I was to be but couldn't see it. I needed to keep looking, all the while leaving behind me a trail of drawings and paintings, a trail of indicators and proof of genius.

While I worked on painting in that little trailer far back on the Santa Barbara home property, I held, like a protective medal, the first painting reminding my hand and eye that I knew intimately where the magic came from, and how it felt to 'river' through me.

M.

Now I am a young old man, sitting in the sun waiting for the angry world to take from me all that I love. And then to make me wait a long short time for my death.

First we discover that little comes unless you are wide awake, prepared to deny the system at every turn. Then we are slapped to understand, no one granted us permission.

If we accept that we have been 'bad' with this life, took liberites and embarassed people, squirted the vile juice of presumption on anything which crossed our path, then we are cursed to a skin-peeling loneliness and hungry sense of wasted life.

If, however, we embrace the entire history of that tangled life of anti-authoritarian presumption and separate it from the accusations and punishments of the present, there are oceans of past harmonies to carry us smiling to our graves.

Such has been my painting life, an ocean of harmonies. May be that the evidence has no lasting value to others, but to me much of it still holds the power to levitate. So paint I will til I can no longer do it.

N.

Is any of this true? I do not care so long as the record reflect what actually happened. Truth in these modern times is for sale or available at the fear and loathing deli.

Reminiscence is time travel of the best sort, allowing the accounts to be settled with bullies, villans and the disrespectful. But settlement doesn't work unless it come bathed in the curious fluids of one-way forgiveness.

While the painting early on carried me solidly forward, flirtations with music, theater and dance teased expectations. Early sixties my school music instructor was a kind and generous man of cattle ranching heritage named Brubeck. I was in high school and focused on folk music, Elvis and the Beatles. We had no clue about the deeper aspects of Jazz. One day our teacher had his brother come to play piano and talk to us. The music was like several waterfalls unexpectedly criss-crossing in repeating splashes of harmony and counterpoint. It was way beyond anything we had ever experienced. What stayed with me all these years was the exotic mix of man and music, seeming so completely dependent on the visible structures of math. Now Dave Brubeck is gone and I'm supposed to tell people this story. Dave Brubeck came to a high school in Santa Barbara, California, and talked to us kids! He talked to me. And I listened.

But not with my young self. I listened with my old self. Now I realize it was one of those turning moments when I was given glimpses of the structural and reactive magic that would carry my sensibility for a long life. Set the limits, trust yourself to feel the invisible walls and rules, select the colors and syncopation, allow that the math of it all become music - become magic stripped bare.

Inside the Brubeck story is the answer to the question of this pretend book. How do we survive life? Some laugh and say no one survives life and I say how sad for you to believe that. Devote religious folk believe they survive life - and because they believe it they do survive. True heroes survive life. Legends are all about life after life. Recovered drunks and recovered addicts survive life. Nelson Mandela has survived life but unfortunately so has Adolf Hitler. Artists have a chance at surviving life, but much rests with how they regard their own creativity. Dave Brubeck most certainly survived life. Next question and a lot trickier, 'how do we live with survival?' I say the answer rests with memory.

O.

There is comedy in most things and to know it, see it, feel it and use it is to spread the wings of your life as far forward as you do back. It is implicit in the indecency of those magical people who live beyond the point where their loss to us would have been tragically useful. Imagine James Dean as a miserly old crank or Marilyn Monroe as a bitchy, sad, old hag. Betwixt all of that is the greatest comedy, the poignant paradox of the invention of our druthers.

I find myself wondering if I haven't lived longer than is decent. Though small and insignificant, I carried a torch for the possibilities of life. The flame's low now, and I am left with this clumsy process of recording what went into my small life, both the lies and the truth of it.

Last night I was reading Pessoa's *Book of Disquiet* and marvelling at his mental gymnastics or bendings, how he pushed so much aside for the sake of justifying his choice to live in an unwarranted social prison of his own design. A comedy really, of Heidegerian proportions. I feel a love/hate relationship with his writings.

But this morning, awake at dawn with the twin realizations that, first, against so many odds I am still alive - and second that the weight of complete and utter ruin is fast upon me, I reach cautiously for any thread I might cling to in this darkness.

Though I worked hard at denying that publication would ever define me, I lost that effort, because here I sit devastated by how this fall from grace destroys my soul, and angry that I allowed it to happen. That the good and honorable work of four decades to support that which I completely believed in would, in the end, destroy me and those I love. It is worse than bad, uglier than tragic, it is the blackest joke.

And yet. The only way forward with this history as good load is to reinvent how all of the content is to be delivered. What will people pay for? So I focus as hard as I can and the squeezings send me back beyond the business into those formative times...

The exhibition was across the bay in Oakland. The paintings of Jules Pascin. From the minute I entered the exhibit space I was floating in his gossamer thin washes of arabic colors tangled around the forms of beautiful, short-haired women of the nineteen-twenties. Their poses laid back at three quarter angles as though the couches had been tipped up to Pascin's advantage. Each portrait belonged, all together all of that sweet short Jew who loved with his eyes. And he's a secret still which is very fine with me. Love the secret of him and his completions, how he blended Paris and the Carribean.

It is the Pascins, the Marins, the Morandis, the Tom Thompsons, the Don Weygandts, the Wolfgang Carlbergs, The Bonnards, the Jose Sabogal's that thrill me to the bone. They and so many other under-sung painters, along with all the great fermenting unpublished poets, all hold up man's truest and best livelihoods and the sacred ceremonial examples they are. Therein lies one of the best set of histories - there is where we have always been offered pathways to survival and dignity.

This then is the answer to the question: 'why do I bother if all that I create is destined for obscurity?' Pathways to survival and dignity, investments in best hopes for mankind. The ultimate reward plus obscurity.

P.

This writing moves along like a drunken old camel on hash-hish; a skip here, a foot dragging there, a leap across an imagined terrible canyon, all while chewing invisible fodder and snorting laughter at remembered jokes. There is never any risk that someone will mount this camel and use it for transport. Instead the drunken camel is the stuff of crazy, campfire stories.

Four years old I recall that black and white pinto rocking horse my father made for me. I rode it for a thousand miles of adventures and job interviews convinced that any second my baby-self would kick the rockers off and truly gallop to muscial horizons of cattle and natives and nice girls. I found those horizons and at least one superb nice girl / magnificent woman, life partner. But that came much later. Before that were fish and goats and cotton-top marmosets. All that glue that holds the scales to my soul. Before that I made mistakes, it is fortunate for the world that I was never in charge of anything. Send me into the burning building for the children but never leave me to make big decisions. Art sick.

And there were Phil and Sylvia two elegant little, old people rapturously in love on into late life. He the rapscallion, she demur and helpful. When he died she went lost and then angry and mean, a complete metamorphosis from butterfly to dirt-eating snake because you see, Phil was never supposed to die, leastwise not before her. Somethings, some things, in life are the absolute co-joining of life and species. We are not meant to fully understand, we are given the opportunity to see completely but that does not assure understanding.

And what I see this morning is the memory of the neighboring orange grove with its pervasive metalic incense, We fifteen and fourteen year old boys spent a summer's week digging an eight foot by eight foot hole five feet deep. Then we dug a tube-like tunnel from that hole's bottom, running twelve feet and coming up in Ronnie's yard. Our soon to be hideout hole was just inside the large citrus orchard. We planked across the top with old lumber and covered that with a few inches of loose dirt.

Ronnie and his family moved away. But others joined me in regular meetings in the "fort." Inside we carved alcove-like shelves in the walls and set up candles for light. Everything in there had to be brought in through the long skinny tunnel. We spent a lot of time down in, discovering ourselves, until other distractions took us away.

We heard about the accident second-hand. Happily the farmer was not hurt when he and his tractor fell through the roof of the "fort." He had been discing his orchard. I worried for a couple of years that I would be discovered and jailed. Never told that story til now. Occasionally I wonder how lucky we had been that none of us were in that hole when the tractor came crashing in.

Q.

Forty seconds of wondering after meaning and then the mind rolls over to reset its comfort to a false empty. Handy device if that same mind be prone to ripping itself to shreds with Barracuda-like memories sauced over by 'what ifs': every thought a repeat, every sentence a duplicate of the one before. Walking back through experience is the only way to find what is fresh and new. Observations of observation - the recording of recording. The abstractions aren't. Reality is. But then damnably the writer observes himself out of life - so busy paying attention that attention is lost. So busy watching for the next step that this step is never felt, so pleased to notice that the coming emptiness is always a surprise.

With the threats of collapse, we are ready to be in collapse and it is 'clear' to us that all is lost. Though of course, nothing is lost yet save for clarity. And when the sun shines on our interiors we are ready to believe in accomplishments as yet unknown. When as life and memory rewinds us, none of that compares with the richness of the actual.

It was the sixties. Signed on to work a communal farm up Comptche Road in the Mendocino Redwoods and fell in rapturous love with forest, jersey cows, chickens and sticky - sweet - wasp- infected - windfall-strewn fruit orchards. But the crowding of lazy, spoiled, naked, people had me leave for the woods of Fort Bragg to live with a woodcutter's large family. Here I learned to fall trees and work dangerously far beyond fatigue. I learned to eat out of a garden and cook on a massive old wood range.

Then I heard of a job available pulling line on a small commercial trawler. It was a two man boat, harbored at Noyo. Old, slow, greasy, wrapped around a hold for the catch and a cantankerous Cummins marine diesel. Vince was the owner and operator of this oily, barnacled, rusted, happy tub of mistakes; he was large, fat and slow and seemed only as alive as was absolutely necessary.

Because I had no experience, I got five dollars a day plus grub and a small percentage of the catch. I'd never fished at sea let alone commercially. The draw for me was a chance at defining adventure.

We had made a couple of short day trips, fishing primarily for salmon and with only modest luck. Vince decided it was time, and I was ready, to go for a long run out and north, perhaps to Alaska. We'd fish until we had to go to port to sell and supply. Then go out again, moving up the coast to new ports each time.

This was the middle of the twentieth century yet we had no electronics, and no radio. Vince had spent his adult life at sea and knew navigation. I was young, strong, stupid and moderately willing. It was summer and my short time at sea had filled me with a salty thrill, I seemed born for the expanse and the vagaries. No motion sickness, no loneliness, no fear of the deep, none of the usual self-preservation that would keep a man on the land. The ocean said every second that I didn't matter. That had me drawn up within my thin shell where I smiled and arranged my cautions like a school girl arranging cosmetic bottles. The ocean had no way of knowing that, at eighteen, eight county doctors looked at the results of two weeks of cruel and painful neurological testing and told my black-haired mother I had three years maximum to live. The ocean didn't know that this commercial fishing venture might be my last taste of life as stretched. What power does certainty have when you are certain that certainty is beautiful in its powerlessness?

In the evenings, especially moonlit, when the ocean found its idle speed of slow roll, the blackened wet surface shimmered and lied to us, speaking of mass and substance enough to hold the boat protected, to hold us atop its pillowy deceit. It was gelatinous, not liquid. Whenever a leaping fish or leviathin broke its surface the display was purest magic, impossible. Ropes of pearls drawn up and allowed down, no spray all spangle, defining the clash of time signatures and of torn sound. Oily wet, a mad glistening.

I don't recall the names of the parts and places on that old boat. There was a sunken walkway along both sides and the stern, deep enough to have me standing top of my thighs. If I turned towards the center of the boat, the center of the boat raised to just below my waist and contained a hold full of ice, the place for the catch. Facing out, winches handled hauling in the heavy lines which fed up the poles. Standing down in that sunken walkway, sidewall of the boat to lean against, the limitless ocean seemed to rise chest high as I gazed across its dancing surface. There were all manner of cable and ropes and sharp tools to navigate, a challenge in a calm sea. When I walked to the very front of the boat, a couple of steps had me up slightly in a kind of caged crow's nest. I enjoyed standing there, leaning in the ship's direction and feeling the struggle of forward motion.

It was of a morning when the sky inhaled and held its breath. Some female force far distant took hold of the edge of the sea and flipped it up just once while pulling taught. The water, in a drawn-out minute, went to a dead calm. Just like a sheet of glass far beyond eyesight. Black and silver and green beneath the ocean, laid down as if hiding in wait of instructions.

The old trawler chugged, burbled and popped forward but it felt has though we weren't moving. Earily the ocean's surface crept, without a wrinkle, ahead of us; crept to match the forward crawl of the boat. Back behind, the wake rippled briefly before being sucked flat by the calm. Even with the engine noises constant, all I experienced was silence. And the light, that peculiar crystal clear dark light, illustrated the silence. High off in the distance a black wall of cloud forced the sun's light to button-hook off the upper atmosphere and splay out, without feature, to a blackened luminescence. Time collapsed in on itself. Part of me was at rest and in comfort with the sensation. A smaller part of me, like a tiny internal weather station, was apprehensive and anxious for some, any preparation. But for what?

R.

"How are you?"

"Me? Why, I'm full of myself. But still able to appreciate that you have a ways to go yet."

Stories are like socks. The good ones, anyway. All that goes to make the closed open-ended tube is container and/or protective housing. It is that which it might contain, the space inside which waits, that's the nameless stuff - the future cargo - the rationale. Stories and the socks go nowhere without the locomotion of needs applied from outside.

S.

Dead calm is what the old sailors call it. The ocean as a flat piece of glass, part mirror, part slate. But those words do not encompass the shock and disorientation, the tangible sense that an explosion of cosmic proportions is building, that the human heart cannot withstand the tension except if the brain ride ahead to prepare for landing or the heart turn itself over to the nameless corner of spiritual stasis where nothing is required, nothing expected, nothing applied for.

The painter in me chose looking, chose looking hard, chose the demand for accurate record because understanding was impossible. I looked, racing across that expanse of glistening flat, table-flat, out across until there was nothing to see but the pulsing mirageaic horizon line. I looked hard ahead, blinked, turned and did the same thing in each direction. Except for the slow dance of the sky it was the same in all directions. And, though the boat's motor chugged, it felt as though we were standing still.

"This is weird Vince. How long will it last?"

"Hours or days, can't ever know. But when it gets ready to change it won't tell us, it will slap the shit out of us and quick."

"So, what do we do?"

"I idle the boat and make sandwiches. You pull in all the rigging. These calms usually creep out the fish and they dive til something changes. Most times anyway."

A day and a half later I detected the very slightest carpet of ripple on the vast ocean surface. Saw its dappled sparkle before I felt it. Saw the boat actually moving before I felt it and the sounds changed. They went from hollow metallic to nearby and a recognizable normal. Like clearing your ears from a rapid plane descent.

Plugged and then unplugged. Dense and instantly freed. Thick to airy. Leaving a loud pulsing smoky party room to walk out into a cool openness, dark and ticklish.

But the memories could not hold, as today's worries suck the life out of any backward's view, sap the strength of reflection, gag the Barstow, throttle the Pacoima, pinch off silliness into small bites of too salty, too loud, too worrisome, too heavy.

"Like, you could truly pull it off. It's you. Too you. You could, like, grow it out really long. Tie it back and do the ramped-up bang thing."

"You're talking to no one, talking and not saying a thing…"

Ah, so we were finally moving, because now all of my senses were affirming it. In that time of transition, that full-horn-chorus of 'Okay,' I allowed myself to look harder at where I was, at the dark, oily sheen atop the peeling paint and rusted crust of the old boat. There was that separation, the oily and the coarse rust. It was as if this boat has its own form of eczema, a road-surface gravelly growth. On Vince it was hard to tell where his eczema started or the dirt ended. And the man's oiliness was as if he oozed WD-40 out his pores.

I noticed these things and then I noticed the cracks in handles, the frayed ropes, the buckets of garbage, the fish guts and torn rain gear. Fear set in as I figured out that this, in reality, was a piss-poor excuse for a ship and we were on the high sea with no land in sight.

A slice of bright light shot through the piling clouds and blinded me to distraction, just enough to enjoy an increasing roll to the water's surface, just enough to change the subject.

Raindrops. Wind pushed through and then quit, then came again. Quit again. Boat rolled sideways. Suddenly, as a big wave

swam against us, Vince turned the ship to face the waves and hollered instructions at me. The sky darkened further but now with
Bierstadt linings to the roiling clouds. Moments before we had been
in a dead calm?

So much happening fast, all of it with an immersible drama and
symphonic beauty. Fear left me as though a drain plug had been
pulled. I stood and turned slowly, arms outstretched to pull in the
light rain. Eyes were drawn by the light shafts, carving the swelling
rounded clouds. As the waves grew larger, Vince guided the boat up
the face of an approaching one. The diesel burbled and, though we
moved slow, the oncoming wave, at twice the speed, rolled us up
and down and away. Putted and burbled up the dark walls of the
now towering waters until the brow of the old boat stuck up in the
air above the frothed wave top and stalled for a long second. The
water moved past and the boat rocked precariously forward and
slammed down on the backside of the departing wave once again to
burble and putt, but now the sea took on its own sounds roaring in
compressed argument, screaming at itself, completely unforgiving.
The sound of a world full of blinded wrestlers set loose on a universe
of birthing females while old motors ran away in reverse to find the
release of explosion.

All of my life I have been able to turn off sounds, like hitting
some sort of mute button. And now, fascinated by the inverted
tempest, I looked side to side and saw how it was that the flashes of
light made momentary mirrors of opposing wave walls. I watched
our boat reflected and saw how she crept down the receding wave,
down into the trough. And, for a moment, terrified, I watched as
the nose of the craft dug down into that armpit of the sea as though
determined to move straight down and under. Next oddly and
miraculously, the boat's nose rose up the oncoming wave as its butt
hung in the departing wall of water. Looking at the mirror wall, I

could see under the boat and, as my eyes moved up, my own silouette and that of Vince in the pilot house, chewing his cigar and
holding the helm. We hung there, level and connecting the bottoms of two waves until the rear released and slammed down into a
proper verticality. Putting and burbling commenced and we slow-
crawled up the next wave. The swelling sea and the stormy sky were
all Beethoven, but the silly fishing boat, with its ridiculous noises
and rolling and slapping and crawling action, was like an old cartoon soundtrack. I was enjoying the understandable, even accessible,
comedy of our ride when a pebbly-pink, flying miniature dinosaur
smacked me in the face.

T.

The talking man stumbles and falls and the rush of words slide
sideways to a pileup. Something illusive triggered a low grumbling
anxiety attack and the cockroaches of formalism and structure
picked at his brain.

"Don't speak that way! Never write that way! Write this way.
Add your figures so they apologize to one another, never so they
simply accumulate. Evidence everything by implicit acceptance of
formal rule or the cockroaches will carry you off."

Sorry old Stegner would never allow that his admonitions and
absolutisms ever be called such. He struggled to his dying day to
defend his church of the right way. His church of the "vulgar short
story surprise." He convinced himself that those contrivances he
abhorred weren't a large part of his contrived struggle to polish his
words until all semblance of dirty sincerity be made to obey. And so
he guaranteed that which he thought he fought against. It was not
irony it was waste.

Writers should be wary of long spells of productive solitude - these produce secret rationale and false courage. they may be more destructive than excessive drink.

U.

The segments of this novel, this tortured set of remembrances blended with silly theorum and tossed with bouquets of red, red lies, it would seem, are randomly delineated by odd numerical and alphabetical monikers which have no value other than to sectionalize chunks of effort for the author's ordering. So what? I could just as easily have given this novel a confusing set of obviously descriptive chapter headings or obliquely poetic handles. But none of that works here as 'wave-aways.' Best that they appear out of time and on top of reason. Squarely on top.

The Storm Ballet

The flying fish were raw pink cigar shapes with wings. They didn't fly so much as flip through the air as though tossed out of the sea. I ducked as a couple of dozen seemed aimed at my head. Pink splats across the dark sky.

Then they were gone. Followed immediately by hundreds then thousands of flying tuna. Silver blue green taut elipses of fish muscle slicing up out of the rising rolling sea and truly flying in tight arcing formations to slice back into the front wall of the oncoming wave. All open eyes! All wide dotted circles!

On both sides of the burbling old boat, as it rode up and down the tall mammalian-like waves, there were walls of tuna swimming and flying along side us. I was struck dumb by the scene, by the dance. The sky blue-black and darkest green, clouds defined by silver edges of electric light, all of it randomly releasing momentary shafts of luminescence as a stage lighting which tickled the sides of the large fish to make them a coin-hung wind chime chased by roped pearls of trailing water. I spun slowly to look all around me. I was on stage in the middle of this grand production of nature, me neither dead nor alive but gratefully suspended inside of the musical math and chaos of nature's exaltation, allowed there as a record-keeper, as a cosmic accountant, witnessing the internal corrections of a bio-universe which rejects, violently, any form of suspense accounting. Here now, in this egg-beater of a storm, we sat absorbing, only surviving because of our insignificance, only surviving because we had no net effect on the accounting.

A dozen tuna and flying fish flopped on the hold cover soundless until I realized that the roar of the storming ocean had absorbed all secondary sounds. the ambient sound of the violence lay over everything else and drowned it all out.

I looked at Vince in the pilot house and realized by his waving arms and contorted face that he had been screaming at me for some time. Reading his lips, I made it out.

"Rig for tuna, you stupid little bastard!"

Once it hit me that I had been dead to an important opportunity I jumped to action, pulling line, releasing winches, snapping on lures, kicking open bait boxes, scurrying dangerously in the storm's middle, complete with aerial aquatic ballet all round. By the time I went to the otherside, the storm wheezed and subsided to allow the sea normal breathing. And the tuna were gone.

(Later I would conclude that Vince during the storm never once stepped out of the relative safety of the pilot house. I would dream of him in the future, encased in nothing but the wheelhouse, bobbing in a boatless sea, screaming at me, "Rig for tuna, you stupid little bastard!" Slices of bologna stuck by blobs of mayonaise to the wheelhouse windows.)

V.

A wrinkled, browned, flower petal fallen and caught in the cup of the fresh blossom beneath, a narrative moment in nature which argues in arabesque with those academic notions that nature is manifest chaos. It bogles the wide awake and observing mind that the limitless order and math of the biological universe could be seen as chaotic. Though so often trapped in the predictability of patterned motive, certainly human-kind has more claim on the chaotic determinent.

The force that would hold the more and most civilized amongst us to forever protect the most destructive secrets from ever leaving those darkest recesses of our brains, that force would argue that humans may have a capacity for deliberate order, even though any reciprocal capacity for understanding escapes them.

Science used to be about discovery, or at least that was the primary motive. Today the extreme hazard is that science is now primarily a service of government and industry employed to either improve upon nature or put her in her place. Humanity seems to demand, require, expect that nature behave.

W.

Corporations grow to exceed the size of many governments - by size, power and arrogance - while individuals shrink within their shells, becoming less than a particle of their potential selves. Poetics freeze and musicality atrophies. What is to be known of this odd self-destructive species after its gone? So much perverse evidence and so many hideous moral insolvencies.

Art would be the last bastion of humanity's faith in itself, or better said, faith in its potential.

As big band sounds, most worthy and elevated in a black, white and sepia-toned sweep of jerky motions and melancholy, squeezed down to make room for the persistence of improvizational jazz, mass hysteria embraced florid color and hill billy sounds blown through Hollywood horns and car-wash rhythms. There was always the choice between joining in with the mountain of escapees or riding out ahead, alone, and self-innoculated against mediocrity.

X.

Now terrible little vignettes revisit to remind that long ago actions, slow dripping eroding actions of horror, created this worthless silly excuse for a human being - or - that the careful building, organizing, creating steps of these last 5,000 years have proven that the intrinsic strength of each human, that elemental, deeply known, curiously musical and perfectly colored self, will want out to triumph over the evil. That better self will walk out of the woods properly gathered unto itself, clear in its trajectory towards goodness, beauty, usefulness and applied dignity.

Y.

Heroics require all the condiments linked-lives can provide. Lichen-less rocks beg regret or thicker imaginations. And trees bound from within as much as from without. Beauty insists that lichen, rocks, imagination and trees intertwine romantically inside Nature's math and demand, all heedless of audience, pause, or pending trauma.

On another commercial fishing trip, rigged for salmon, the bell on the end of the outrigger rattled hard - then still - then hard. Vince indicated I needed to pull in all the lines. From things he'd told me I figured we had a seal on. One which had tried to steal a salmon. Turned my stomach to think I would be hauling in a hooked seal that Vince would have me dispatch.

It was on the very last line, nothing else was hooked. The winch was full and I had to haul in the braided line with gloved pulls. At first it felt like dead weight. Then nothing. Easy pulling. Must'a come free. Then tough again; loose, tight, loose, tight, loose again. I quit pulling and Vince hollered to keep at it.

I looked over the side of the boat as I yarded in line, careful to wrap the coil away as he had cautioned. I couldn't see anything, then came a dark oval well down in the water. What I saw next fascinated me. It was a string of pearls edging that dark oval. And all of a sudden it raced up and out of the sea, right at me! I leaned back and as I fell I heard the crack of Vince's rifle.

We had hooked a seven foot blue shark and it had seen me long before I had noticed the dark oval of its mouth. The string of pearls had turned out to be small sharp teeth, hundreds of them.

Vince's shot had killed the beast. It was my job to muscle it, with help of a winch, onto the deck. It was to go to a Chinese restaurant customer.

Replay replay replay. Shark, mouth open, gaining speed, directed at my head, prepared to harvest me in pieces. Tiny eyes, killing mouth, its entire self encased in a rubbery sack of skin which barely hid its roiling thrashing need to be in its next body. Caught between itself, caught and forced to play out, caught in absolute vehemence.

I had been the bait. I, the goat staked out for the predator. I the expendable one. Had it all gone wrong for me, Vince would have rolled my remaining pieces into the sea and headed back to port for another idiot, (perhaps this next time he would succeed in avoiding the romantics).

The sea will turn your self on your self and time will swell in the recesses, the scripts played forward leak into terrorized cracks, forming false connections. So I was to imagine Vince being the one rolled into the sea and I at mysterious controls completely oblivious of what to do, what direction to head, how to survive the adventure turned to death.

Back to port, back to Noyo Harbor, he said 'get your stuff ready in a couple of days we head out, will be gone a month or more.'

Found myself splitting firewood for my host family and thinking of the return to the sea. Hatchet in hand, kindling the goal, I felt my right wrist deflect off something that wasn't there, something resistant. The sharp blade went to my left hand, the one holding the wood, and sliced the skin on the back to a perfect fillet, exposing bones. Doctor said, you won't be using this hand for many months. To this day scar remains. Never went back to sea. Don't even know what happened to Vince. Don't want to know. That's how some of us handle horrors and peripheral fears, hold them off - save yourself for those times when once again the shark is aimed at your head.

Z.

The Talking Man talks. He's not reminiscing, thinking about what went on before. He's talking his way through the scrap-yard of his brain, through the saved bits of experience and mounds of lies he has told himself, talking man. Only now, he's not trying to sort for the truth, he's determined to catalog orally, what the hell happened.

"Where ya been?"

"Been everywhere. You won't believe where I've been. Likely you don't want to know."

"No, that's not true I do want to know."

"Well then let me tell you that I've been to harmony and back more times than I can count."

"Alone or was someone with you?"

"Both."

"And how do you rate harmony?"

"Thumbs up. Great place, but you're screwed if you choose it as your goal. It's a place you pass through on your way towards those goals your presumption demands. Harmony is out there, everywhere. Just don't try to pin it down."

Harmony as piece of mind not as peace of mine, let alone mind. Stupid turn of phrase. Not worthy of this restless brain, working as it does to keep moving out away. Keep spreading the edges of the net out beyond the oil-slick of this scatter-shot life.

Form and function, shape and movement, held and holding, blood and bleeding, love and loving, sight and seeing, fruit and fruiting, held and dropped.

The old third tier poet said, 'when my colleagues speak of their writing for a time far beyond their own, I say "I hope you feel better tomorrow."

He said, I said, they said, we pretended to hear and Pessoa walks umbrella in hand to his clerical office allowing himself to think only about his deepest set interiors, secure in knowing neither Balthasar nor Rabelais, had they lived at this his time, would ever notice him at all. For Pessoa there never were any tiers, nor tribes, nor club membership. He gave no service to form and/or function. He was a book-keeper of his own sensibilities, carving for it all the widest variety of the truest of fictions. He took his own confessions.

So I borrow that from Pessoa. This is me taking my own confessions - and knowing in the bargain that I doubt I will absolve myself. Long have I disparaged the nonsense of the sanctity of forgiveness. I will not forgive Hitler, nor Cheney nor the Serbian butchers nor the CIA nor Monsanto nor the casually dressed billionaire morons of San Jose. Forgiveness must have its place but I don't even want to know what that is.

(Turns out the man was so smart he invented ways to cancel out his own value, his own seat on the bus. And others came quickly to steal that invention, dip it repeatedly in the goo of easy, thrilling access and serve it to the masses at five dollars a throw. Those thieves, they die now wondering after their own decay. And the masses lose first their peripheral vision, later their sense of smell and finally any memory of love.)

It came too mean, it came to mein, it came to me. So many of the cruel stupidities came out of instinctual necessity, of a corrective plan. We have always looked too close and not close enough. Matriarch vs. Patriarch, the contest is a thread throughout time. Neither side to be picked. Worse yet are those cancerous efforts to merge genders. Appetite must cease to be used as rationale, as apology, as discovery. Appetites are of limited value as peripheral evidence. Mammalian survival is the key. To save - and why - that is the compunction that must be understood.

And the frauds of it all; beginning with the trust in instinct rather than knowledge, in experience without recipe, in a gardener's after-thought, of exaggerated epiphany, of humor's tow, of reverie's aside.

Now, I begin to understand the complete horror of my father's loneliness. He could never slow the construct of his walls. He was forever someplace else. A horror without threat, without familiarity. The deepest horror of endless wait.

The only way to beat the wait is to finish each project and product and move on to the next. Leaving completed evidence is the way to deny anyone a clear trail. Process has power but never so much as product. And any product true to itself is candidate to become icon.

Recognize the 'wait' for what it is, prelude to death and then - only then - deny it by always racing through life without mirrors, without the backwards glance, without forgiveness, without lingering apologies. And that race must run from completion to completion, never allowing others to deflect or slow.

i.

The sleepy eye followed the faltering hand until an entrance appeared and the story spilled out, a herd of ants flooding through the opening. And behind that tired cats waited for sadness to harden.

San Francisco in the sixties, beginning before Leary and Kesey, was all black and white and tea green mixed with chalky milk. The shadows oozed out beyond their edges. Glen Yarborough sang in a sound like liquid graphite and pushed Johnny Mathis into a bald yet pretty self-embrace.

Did I write of the Russian district? Where large-boned eternally middle-aged women wore aprons like social armor? And beards were not dissimilar from armpit hair? And ferment was a cooking stasis? And the food was reason to volunteer to never question, never leave, never rise above. All of it too potatoey to avoid. If you escape it is by accident, wandering off in a fat brain stupor until the ocean's magnetic pull reintroduced choice. The Russian district which the world would come to know, overnight, as Haight Ashbury; the Russian district where curling, flacking Victorian paints acted like velcro to the wandering Pacific fogs, holding the moistures in service to doldrums until that one night when everything changed and LSD replaced sauerkraut and weed replaced vodka and street merchants learned to make change backwards.

Same time frame: Tina Pushkin and her transparent, ancient, ballerina grandmother, smothered in heavy drapes in that old frame house on 48th Street; Tina who kept the Czar's memory alive for her Babushka, Tina who wanted to believe a real world would some day wash her clean of Russia. Instead, after I left, it was a candle fire that destroyed the house, killed the old ballerina in her bed - the framed picture of the Czar by her side, and sent Tina to spinning madness.

Oh, you liar, she says, it was never like that. But how would she know, she's not been in my head?

ii.

There are fogs of different consequence playing out the sounds and looks of memories. Sometimes what happened twenty-five years ago feels all the world like it happened fifty years back and vice versa. And how curious is the filter which assigns greater or lesser value to periods which, though chronologically akimbo, feel older or younger?

When I first set eyes on the love of my life, the two green jewels that are her eyes pulled my internal longings out of my head and splayed them across my beard and belly. I had no beard then but my trickster memory recalls the sticky sweet mystery of her exotic beauty holding chin hairs in odd twists as my own eyes screwed deeper into my head to hide from the inadequacy I tortured myself with. Young as she was, I was no match for her poise, her native intelligence, her absolute spiritual power. I was captivated, I was catapulted, I was entranced. From that moment my each and every truest thought of love was of her.

To think now, after decades of my mistakes and roaring stupidity I could have her in my arms still, as we wobble into the grandest of old ages, it is clearest evidence that one gift of fullest maturity is the chance to inhabit memories in reverse. I knew as a boy that I might, might, might know such incredible comfort and happiness as an old man. I remembered myself forward and perhaps the artist in me made it so, perhaps the fiction writer as tactician made it so, perhaps the pounding insistence that sincerity is beauty and fertility incarnate, perhaps I had nothing to do with it, perhaps this grand late life has come soley by her efforts, perhaps my stupidities were no match for the staying power of her faith and love. So I remember forward and it lays a blanket to platform the remaining years, before this life rolls into a fat, final enchilada, oozing at every opening and edge. Those fogs of consequence have carried life to useful and appreciated best days.

iii.

Summer of '68. Mendocina, California and the redwood forests. Ocean and tree smells folding together like a Dvorjak string quartet. Back then the vistas and envelopes of wind-directed sight and longing were set loose by the outside of this splendid place. From city and suburb to here was a passage through the prismatic boundaries between nature's nature and man's growing toilet.

The place was prelude to the commercial fishing experience (more akin to playing small time pirates than any form of commerce). When off the boat I stayed with the Dougherty clan, husband wife and ten children, one on the way. He, a massive jovial dunce of a man free, completely free, of the ravages of requitted thought. His entire life was his working and his loving. He was a woodcutter, firewood his game. Every day five days a week, he set his sights on cutting and splitting a cord of wood, over 250 cords a year to sell. On weekends he did whatever it took to help his wife with the subsistence gardening, butchering, fence mending, canning, smoking of meats, and repairing their ramshackle house.

His neck and head all the same width slightly narrower on its flat-topped top. His shoulders sloped a long ways down to the tangle of exaggerated arm muscling. When he walked nothing moved from waist up. His feet pointed straight forward in spikey, heavy caulk boots. I wondered if all those thousands of hours packing chainsaw and supplies into the woods hadn't somehow thickened his torso to immobile - until I saw him scramble up atop massive fallen tree trunks with fifty pounds of burbling, deadly McCullough saw, chain sharpend to resemble those light-activated shark's teeth.

Terry was proud of one thing, his family, but mostly as an appointment kept by his manhood. Ten children in ten years. NO beat skipped. All healthy, especially mama Molli. Somewhere he had figured out it would be a clear sign of his success as a man if he begat in obvious powerful and regular fashion.

Molli was a Dorthea Lange stoic in a perpetual smiling cloak. Plain, strong, and fully smart with her own gratitudes. She was built for motherhood, built for self-sufficiency and ripe for Jerry. Ecstatic to find that her small world offered overlaps of constant good challenge.

This half century later I cannot picture her, but I feel her steadiness and watchfulness and contentment. Her large garden crawling with careful children, picking bugs and thinning plants while they giggled and sang. All summer long, supper came from a giant wok on her enormous wood cook range (built for a logging camp) from which came the day's stir fry of venison or fish in with the garden's bounty - sweet edible podded peas, chopped cabbage, carrots, potatoes, onions, greens of all manner. This over brown rice - one of the few purchased food items. Same menu yet slightly different each day

- fresh tuna I brought from the boat or Jerry's venison, a chicken no
longer laying eggs - whatever the protein always framed ecstatically
by Molli's fresh garden harvest. Those children knew no other way-
though poor as church mice, Molli and Terry gave them the richest
possible young lives.

iv.

IV, intravenous or the number four. Allowing what I wrote to
transport me back to the Dougherty summer. I find the words work
but I know its only for me. Because I was there and it takes so little
to return me to that yeasty dream-like Tom Bombadil time. A time
that was all answers no questions. A time that was deliberate and
aimless in an animal sort of way. A time that was a salad-like middle
to accidental parenthesis. It was symbolic of nothing, it supported
nor aknowledged no governance or religion; it sat still as a best
time could while constantly blooming. It was a restful time for the
brain. Aniticipations deflated there. Anxieties became giggles, tight
muscles wiggled and the outer layers hung on for fleeting moments,
unnecessary and thin.

Some lives intersect with slicing, cutting, burning surety. And
they return randomly to suck joy and comfort from the least of us.
But so what? If we allow this we are this. And in that is corrosion
and unmaintained inventory and babies who are named too late for
it to matter.

Sentimentality and romance, though particulate embarrassments which slow us for the bullets of evil's worst thrust, would also
cradle us in slow beats and warm liquids sweet with innoculating
substance. These split-screen times pretend to give us, in the whole,
a view of life's true poverty and vulgarity while they disguise the fact

that the meanest souls amongst us decide every moment what we would see and how it does hold and sell and push and round back again. The largest most generous souls amongst us, though charged with pulling babies from burning buildings, must also never quit arranging flowers, scripting songs, capturing visions of splendid beauty and romance, for in the deepest sentimentality is the most fertile of nature's answer to wastefulness and emotional insolvency. There I said it. Shoot your damn shit-charged guns at me, I am, if not protected, at least ready in my best tear-stained humors.

v.

The distance from deepest despair to the loft of certain success is a wink of an eye; but only if one is prepared to see and accept the turn, the promise, the change. The lower depths render limbs old and feeble, the ascendancy to promise of hope winds those same muscles taught for exertion. Therein lies some universal law of physics in marriage to, or in obedience to, the absolutes of outlook; as if to say a body in motion is always subordinated and colored by the mind of that body's outlook. Know it to be slow and it slows, know it to be in glorious flight and it moves well beyond itself.

We hold these truths to be self-actuated; that all men are capable of creation, that all men are known to be known and unknown, and that building it does not make it so. For in the will is the first light of all creation, only if that *willer* unplug, drop out, and trust his zone completely. For the crutches crutch but the walkers don't walk and without recognition of these addendums to truth we are but limited. Limits only ever belong to the limited.

To die while you are still alive, that is the wish. To die while you are dying that may be the fear. None of which is to be known unless undoing be the choice. And to undo, that is the waste and the wasting.

But to pour over what has been done, known, felt - that is certainly to remain alive and to shield the flame. It is when the lies of reminiscence give personal history changeable colors... but that's talking about the individual.

Society does do the similar, allowing that a set of lies be generally agreed to, otherwise there would be no history.

The individual artifice versus the collective, therein lays the contest of greatest import; may be the fights between decency and regency, between health and wealth, between building and drilling, between fertility and sterilty, between song and wrong, between life and death, good and evil, dance and march, love and own.

We see the humor, we see the humor.

The Third Section of the Book

Thought I was done. That the project and process had found
an emotional conclusion. That my French fountain pen had finally
failed, as its threads crumbled and tortoise shell went thin. But then
I found this German fountain pen, this precise, hexagonal black cylinder with inlaid red stripe. This heavy authoritative writing stick.
And I found that the carriage of this book project still vibrated in
anticipation of adventures wanting to be on a page. The triumphant
adventures of early shapings and manifest joy. The overlaps of birth
and death, hungers and satiation.

What is it about Eugene Delacroix and Pessoa that for me
strikes that ambient structured chord? Two very different men accepting their positions and the forms of its trappings, the dress,
the ritual, tone of relationships, fabric of process, formalities and
escapes. Was it that comfort of accepted lot? Was it the complete
self-identifying embrace of who they found themselves to be?
So we sit old and alive. Struggling yet appreciative. Well prepared to avoid those last waitings that would define an entire life
as wasted. And the tone so well maintained by the wrap of random
revisits to the life before - where the truth of any of it is but burnt
frosting.

Uno

Would the vignettes, the stories within stories, expand now to fill the cavern walls of the remembered times? Could it be time to trust the minutiae of so many details?

As a child I marvelled at the command my heroic father held for details, facts, knowledge. Though my questions back then would have been thin and self-answering, his responses, nonetheless, gave me high shelves to pine for. In retrospect I know it was the sound of his voice, his posture of authority, his deference to the artistic, his well-cultivated agnosticism, his quiet disdain of the feeble-witted, his silence in the company of silliness, and his dry wholly acceptable sarcastic humors. Though raised in rural Wisconsin, fringed during the depression's dry friction with tattered edges, he absorbed the sophisticated manneristic outlook of Jazz Age sashay without the moves, or the jive, or the clothing choices. He was of a type, of the James Stewart, Duke Wayne, Henry Fonda sort. He was Sandburgian, hat in hand and with glances that worked corners. Back in the thirties, if Crosby and Hope always looked as though they had been caught with canaries in their mouths, my father looked as though he was the one who caught them at it. In a room full of men, he likely would have been the one you would pick to be in charge. But you'd never pick him if you were looking to have a good time, he just looked regular to a fault.

He was a writer by desire and practise but never by culmination which was unfortunate for everyone as he had the gifts and the attitude to have joined Steinbeck, Faulkner and Williams as an uncompromising fourth leg.

World War II over and he married to a mature Caribbean beauty, a trip was made to Cuba for one purpose - to have a sit down with his literary hero, Hemingway. As a bonafide, decorated, marine-survivor of the hideous South Pacific 'theater', deep inside he figured he earned some things including an audience with EH. In Havana he'd made the acquaintance of a smooth-talking fancy-dressing guide/gambler/pimp who casually claimed intimacy with Hemingway. That connection proved dangerous. When "Francisco" was caught stealing, my father, fresh from the horror of war and the intensity of human depravity, convinced all and everyone that the thief's life was in jeopardy. Knowing of his desire to find Heming-way, Francisco bargained to take mother and father to the author's lair across the island, this in exchange for his life. On a short leash, the trip was made to a sweaty tavern.

EH was inside, he told them. Hand on his neck, father said - take me to him, introduce us, now. Francisco melted in the wedge and broke down in tears. "But senor he will kill me if he sees me."

The ex-marine entered the noisy bar alone. Papa Hemingway was esconced at the bar with a wide-open area around him. He talked to himself in a stupor. The tavern was full and noisy but everyone gave the infamous writer a wide berth, people and smoke and apprehensions and desires and furniture and small lights and overlapping noises and desperate insistence swirled in tiny overlap-ping circles within a wide slowly circling band that moved counter-clockwise around the destructive heat at the center - the tortured, misaligned, spoiled, suicidal, decaying ego. My father walked into that empty zone and faced EH.

"You! Come here!" spit EH.

Six foot four, former first sergeant for Carson's Raiders in the Pacific, an unwilling witness to the violent deaths of many of his closest friends on bloody beachheads - he stood still and felt a combination of dizzy regard to be in the presence of his literary hero, and combat alertness as he felt a threat.

"Hit me. Hard as you can."

Nothing.

"Hey, farm boy - chicken shit, did you hear me? Hit me hard as you can. Give me your best shot. Now!"

He was screaming.

My father stood still and waited. He was wound to respond, whatever way the moment played out.

Hemingway threw his drink in a wide arc, missing.

In that moment the alignments my father had arranged for his life, the reasoning of his hunger, what he would accomplish with his writing and what that might give him, crumbled down into a growing hole.

He turned and walked out of the tavern without saying a word.

Not enough detail? Obviously this writing is not good enough for those who must be led. It might be for those who have emotional laundry and are in need of a line for that laundry to be hung on.

Both of us writers in spirit, for 65 years he never mentioned his experience with Hemingway until the end. I imagine now that whenever the writer's name came up he fought the urge to look away and shake his head. Such cowardice, he would have thought. Like a Jerry Jeff Walker 'train song,' but the heart hadn't been broken, it had barely been exposed. Instead the whiskey and rum had convinced Hemingway he had notched another humiliation, another bro-mance rape, another bit of myth building. My father knew the deflating truth of it.

Hemingway was a bore who, without editors and publicists,

would never have made the pantheon. Hemingway would have taught Minnesota high school English and cheated at Wednesday night poker, and day-dreamed about raping his students. Perhaps, had that all been true, he would have been happier in the end.

My father, present in all its horror, had never written a word about the war. He couldn't imagine the sort of degenerate who would. Yet, grind out the man and men, he couldn't help himself, he loved 'For Whom The Bell Tolls'.

At 94, loosened by mild senility, he told me six times in 3 days the story of meeting Hemingway and always ended with what a sorry bastard he was.

Art leaks from sorry bastards.

Upended. Appended. What a load of crap this ridiculous book is? But it must be for that is so much of life and storytelling. Especially from an old brain struggling to maintain control of thought and creation.

Hold to sincerety. Give truth a wide berth or let it alone altogether for it doesn't want to be 'told' - it wants to spray out the edges of a swirling tale (or tail), a pattern of oily dots marking for goodness and for nature's math.

To this point, over eleven years of piling on, carving off, collecting and shoving around these thoughts, constructs and manipulated memories, fictionated, all out of necessity and heedlessness. What is the matter of any of it? These are ghosts I speak of, all gone now save for me - and I'm not certain even about that. My peripheries hand me pieces and, if I remain smart, I put them down without too much, if any, thought. Looking straight ahead I half-see movement just back to the sides where my 'reasoning sight' notes motion - light - shape without clear distinction. Snake-like, eyes shaded, I draw that stuff in and set it on the table.

Night time all vision is peripheral and the thoughts which own the night mix and match until absurdities eat on each other. Borges, Beckett, when what is needed is Hopper and Bonnard. There it is. Art as salvation. Ah, the Arabian rug float and flute haunt. But who gets to sit before it? I do. I sit here because my entire life has been at the altar of art. Too easy, when the stupidities and poverty demand center stage, too easy to forget that within the secret math of art is the ascendancy to a smiler's calm.

Morning. The sortings happen. I shed the night terrors and look into my tired patterning brain for indication of both how the coming day should be and how a longer view may be held. And there are no false identities here. Not like my black-haired mother who wore her persona in an odd twist as disguise. Her persona.

Not the sound but the encircling.

Old feet take on shapes, textures and calamity with no regard for diginity's insistence. They twist, contort, die off, crack, flake, ooze, smell, and argue in ways that disgust most folks. The remainder of an old body does much the same thing but with less of a caged character to the visual horrors. It has to be this way. Yet the energetic optimists, the young at heart, they have ways to direct attention away from old feet and squeaking infirmities. They have ways of making all that is seen be about what is felt, hoped for, and prized. Outlook as though it were a human polish.

Tell me a story damn it. I don't want to hear, or read, about filtering life's meaning. I want the name of he who done it, and a description of his face, clothes, motive and hungers. Then I want to see him in action - or being acted upon.

Give me a piece of truth, a small tight separate piece of truth. Please, before I have to leave, give me something that refuses to be led anywhere.

Appears a Bear

They were four hunters in Oregon's Strawberry mountains. The young doctor had married in; the father-in-law along with his new second-wife and her brother were all three at least twenty-five years the doctor's senior. They had split up in organized fashion, each with rifle and a determination to shoot a bull Elk.

He, the doctor, was a short strong capable man, a sophomore in this initiation season with the rigors of outdoor life, and a master with scalpel, ligament and ligature. Anxious to prove himself in the hunter's realm, he held all humors at bay.

Night before they had killed a bull elk, way up and gone on the mountain, a big beast. Darkness and the freezing cold fast upon them, they hoisted the bled animal up into a tree, planning to return early in the morning to finish field dressing. With exhaustion replacing best sense, they went down the mountain never doubting their ability to find their way back to the same spot in the morning.

The next day, confused, they split up to better locate their hunting prize. Our doctor, after a long hour through fog, mist and treed mountain sides, finds the bull elk and lowers it.

He gave only a fleeting thought to the expensive new black wool, Filson trousers he wore as he proceeded to hunker-in to the elk cavity to clean the entrails, remaining after last night's dark work. Certain the others on his party would soon find him, he proceeded methodically to skin and quarter the beast.

Done and still alone, he slung a front quarter over his shoulder and headed back down towards their camp when he smelled smoke and decided to divert to that direction.

When he came on the three of them they were huddled around a generous campfire, no firearms in sight.

"We were worried about you. How'd you get that quarter away from the bear?"

Our doctor friend asked what bear and proceeded to explain how he had found last evening's Elk, lowered it and finished gutting, skinning and quartering.

"You must have been at a different kill. When we walked up to it we saw a black bear hunkered inside the elk cavity eating away. That's why we came down here and built this fire, to ward off the bear."

It came to them, they all smiled in unison.

She said, "Oh my, those black wool pants... it was you. You were the bear! I am so glad we didn't take any fire arms with us."

What the hell. The simple stories are just that. They are simple and the lesson is to take caution with the lessening lest it become lessoning. Verbs to nouns, nouns to verbs. From potatoes to Jerusalem Artichokes, from dried chips to Vodka - it's this season of change as the planet prepares to dispense of the human glut. So we take small comforts in realizing that it was no bear. It was our doctor bent over in black wool trousers, deep in the bloody cavity of a dead bull elk.

No edict here. Even less edit.

Dos

The suspension of disbelief - is it a useful tool or a dangerous practise? We are in an age of wholesale suspension of disbelief. Disbelief comes as a shaking at the core that is prelude to certainty's action. "No, he cannot be dead!" Followed by "we must do something but what?" Chased by "the lesson in this is that..." And with fortune comes "this must change, never again will I (we)..."

But today the collective shudders are gone as we sit together numb, watching the vulgar extents taken to 'carry' us through the inseparables of entertainment and news(?), our disbelief suspended enmasse, but are we believing or accepting or nodding off?

When my father passed on I believed I was prepared - or was it that I had prepared myself to accept it? Now, a few years later, a feeling begins to creep inside of me suggesting the artifice between he and I belonged to an entire swim of denial, of disbelief. He chose to see in me less than nothing or more than everything as his moods required. While I most times required of him a steadfastness that may have only been cruelly suggested by his introversion and insecurity. Long before my needs pulled at him, he had to accept that external praise, reward, credit, aknowledgement, membership, arrival or sense of triumph - earned triumph - was not to be his. There was, to be sure, a few moments when my awards and positions made him proud and gave him vicarious carriage - but those he could not allow long seat.

Inside of this dark midnight, I come to see my relationship with my father as a fountain pen I write with - and I suspect it may be running out of ink. Following the analogy, I can refill the pen or reach for a different pen - but at this late age and growing infirmity the familiarities of this pen are, as with my blood, my itching skin, my old teeth, my ready and best friend memories - I hold them close now. I need them to keep all together.

I recognize this, keep it to one side, and flirt with returns to the wider sweep of thought, of imagination, of immersion in passions for best patterns.

My shudders are not gone. They are becoming painfully regular. But I do hold them at bay when I paint or when I write and often in the midst of farming.

My edge moments watch for the next fountain pen.

Tres

On Guy Place, fourth floor walkup, Victorian pre-earthquake slum tower, San Francisco's old industrial zone, against McCormick and Shilling and the Bay Bridge off ramp, near that hauntingly lovely old mold-yellow cigar factory, I and my paints resided in one of my most memorable years. Nineteen and full of thirty something, convinced I was in the shadows at the center of the universe. It began St. Patrick's Day of 1966.

Crucifixes.

No comings or goings, all residency firmed in connection to hunger, paradoxical musings, flourishes, tight-shouldered haunching, deep-set eyes. I had long thought the time belonged to another and that I was a side dish, a celery stick in his relish tray, an out of place comma in a long looping sentence, a useless small key to a forgotten padlock. Fifty years later I suspect I may have been the main course in what was most definitely my own coming out, where the thousand appointments with answers and new questions only existed to polish my shaky way forward.

Heads; I drew them, painted them, pushed them into aesthetic corners and what squeezed out were the long stretched forms of crucifixes. Giacometti's first lines, but all sure, no tentatives. The airplane shape of Christ's last moments. The drawn out look of pain and suffering's final exhaustion. The pretense, horrid pretense at triumph. And the sacred patience.

There is that danger that, concerned for prelude, we do not see the fullness of the time. the fullness of ourselves. Remembering that time, and seeing its' depth and skinned-over completeness, stripping it of any preludian hesitations, that is where I might discover a way to avoid being absorbed in hesitation by this time today. Always waiting for what is yet to come, that would seal final moments with the cement of regret. To see and feel this time as a fullness, to remember the fullness of THAT time, these experiences will give us this day.

The quality of Frisco's light came from its insistence. On foggiest ocean-shaped days the light kept creeping or oozing in with crystaline determination. It was as if the fog was a cotton blanket riddled by the sparkling pastel particles of that light which would not be denied. It wasn't mixed in but rather reaching in - and when it finally broke through it was all garden-light with a moist softness that said walk with me, turn slowly in my presence, hold me close for far too soon I will go away again. Be assured I will always return, even if I no longer love you or what you have done to my armatures. I, this light, am not here for you. I am here for this wonderful place folding as it does the land and the sea and harboring the exchanging waves of fog and light, the overlaps and tuck-ins of hills and tides and skies and the brocade of patterned moistened sunlight.

Those Bangkokian ocean smells, the way salt water soupified and made acceptable rotting garbage odors stirred with burnt petroleum, powdered with cinnamon, curry, cilantro, skunk oils and dog feces, all of it slow cooked in the steams of the atmospheric indifference. Birds and whales smell it from a hundred miles out to sea, magnetic and repulsive all at once. The secret ingredients in this stew of smells were the insistent humans wearing their enchiladas, spaghetti, chow mein and borscht as they tortured one another with a needy indifference and that Babylonian thirst for confusion and exploded tradition.

Quatro

If San Francisco was my Zurich, my Berlin, my Brooklyn, my Albequerque then Oregon was my Orinoco, my Lolo Pass, my Tanzania, my Belize, my Valhalla Canyon, my Crack in the Ground, my Fossil, my Monument, my Devil's Elbow, my Ash, my Siltcoos, my Santiam, my French Glen, my Flora, my Fauna, my Owyhee, my Seneca, my Silver Lake, my Geneva.

The unknown sweet, moist, leaf-rot cankered, metal wig-wammed, hideehole where the outside, at least then, shaped every damn thing. To go from the center of the universe to a satellite moon, from the crowded frights to the vast inescapables, from the reason to the purpose.

'Neath the odor shadow of Weyerhauser, where all the world is acrid, where glues and steamed wood oils and burnt fuels coat anxieties in determinate poetry, breaths are held until the tunnel's end. These are the conditions and causes which have long escaped the idiocies of collegiate historians bent as they are toward the brittle acolades of surety's pressure cooker of security. Every age, every time, every segment of the human travel has its purgatories of lidded nastiness where thought, breath, sight, memory, movement, pleasure, discovery, anticipation, and comfort are squashed. Where each of us is forced to witness the terrible destruction of others or ourselves, only now it is done with and through phone cameras and pulsing attentive circles of strangers hungry for the grief of others, hungry for the measures of pain, hunger, suffering, loss, poverty, for in its observation they curiously absolve themselves. They cannot jump in the icy water to save the drowning child but they must watch and record. They will not run into a burning building to save someone but with a saleable shock they insist on witnessing all the horror. Their eyes have become portals of poisoned reverse purpose. They do not see to know what is next, they watch to feel that they have owned an experience they are too weak to belong to.

There was a before. Before this time of being told there was that time of knowing. Particulate circumstance held our shape. We were purely of the overlaps. We were, each of us, a universe teased to individual perfection by choices, by trajectories, by swim; only if we listened without thought to the soft carriage of purpose.

There is no proof in utterance, never has been. Humor's missed cues long ago saw to that. The Socratic insult, the Platonic passions, the Shakesperian nonsense, the Faulknerian hoohahs, all cheapest peeling paint, have liscensed scholarship to inanity in its barberchair pursuit of meaning.

Oregon put diapers on the talking man. They absorbed his insolence, his lunacy, his acidity, and bottled his understandings for later.

Oregon did not come to him he went to her for in the abiding moisture was the wide stage of purpled truest adventure. The Firs, Alders, Pines, Maples, mold, moss, decaying leaf intersect laid everywhere in wait for each missed step, each botched kiss, each unacceptable hunger. Always a preventative, a protection against, sometimes a curative for, the Guccivian cancers; for a hundred years, too coarse to swaddle the insouciant hedons.

Read everything and die-a-muddle, keep the words you be at-tracted to, close at hand, and die assured.

Oregon is curvature unto itself, or several. It is the chainmail-like, fishscale-like, peeling paint-like, barnacled moss-like, cir-cumstance which has had light's success and failures push open the hope-enings of uncovered edges, discovered tonalities, subway absence, violin tangled with piano cascades up against the forced lyrics of too late for the bus, too soon for love, too fast to taste, and all of that sprinkled with lemony alder leaves laughing as they fall in the mixed airs of a fall noon.

Looking back now through the frosted ash of this cold-warm time with mathematicians borrowed to set the end-days clock not from biblical prophecy but from humanity's bump and grind with fossil-fueled excesses, we are a nasty itch upon the surface of this magnificent holy experiment we know as earth and she will remove us in her own ways. The hideous arrogance of organized religions, usurped as they have been by the self-aggrandizing board room shrink to single purpose, are stamping this time though they are but cruel asides to the end-game of nature's reclamation. Because of these uncertain certainties, these cold warmths, these abuttments to the useless arc of human history, I look back now to my San Francisco, my northern California coastal paradises and my storied Oregon with a power-full knowledge that we raced over the top of mankind's best possibilities in our depraved insistence upon satiated soul-less class membership. We've thrown away our music, our food, the catalogs of our useful fears, the interiors of our best poverties, the sloughed skins of innocence and the upholstery of fertile pro-gressions. I remember when the refrain "is that all there is?" was an obvious and rejectable rhetorial question. In that time we all knew there was more behind, beneath, before - more than we could ever count, describe, analyze - we knew because we felt it as who we were.

The nature of entitlements change, but not the emptiness they so often guarantee. I think on all the old close soldiers who have lent me their truths as example, the ones who made it all the way, purpose always in hand. And compared this to the easy invite of an aged indolence. I think of the precise woodpile of Barden, the coal forge of Dimick. I think of Drongesen's harnessed horses and Uncle Ephraim's Guernsey cows. We move in purpose and become purpose.

But what of the landscape of purpose? The back drop? The approaching horizon, the airs the lighting, the ground, the orchestra that is plant growth and wildlife tangle, the weather as oxygenated battle, the godscape of new life and sudden death, the fur and slime of all that is around us, how does all this pinch purpose? Some do not. But place waits for its ordained best momentary landscape. Oregon waits in the parking garage of yesterday's convergence with engaged appreciations. It waits until the return of silversmiths and loggers, handmade tents and jerusalem artichokes, mushroom noodlers, moss filters, and purest water outnumbering coagulants, mud, urine, and blood. Water and greenery's lace wait to reclaim from the vapid this land's next marriage to right purpose.

Oregon is one third aquarium and two thirds rock garden, all of it splotched by the mysterious shadows of a billion trees holding in their forest reserve the myriad answers to future's desperate questions. Her truest inhabitants, truest minions, true club members are the rock chucks, badgers, mountain boomers, martins, lynx, coyote and kangaroo rats. The people here keep to climate-controlled automobiles, trucks, houses, shopping centers and synthetic clothing, peering out and into the aquarium or fenced-off rock garden which surrounds them. A coarse and life-embibed few live out in the air, unprotected and stupid in their love match with nature's nature, their laugh-encircled, sweat-salted, blood-candied, wrestling match with the dirty - dusty - wet - suffocating - refreshing - wide - tight - boundless arena of Earth's long answer Oregon, the New Zealand of petrie-dishes, theTanzania of muted drum beats, the Yukon of coverlet passions, the Bolivia of mentstrual massage, the Burma of insect stews, the Pyrenes of tomato-oiled grandparent love. Oregon by virtue of its insistent excess of tangled nature stands ready to swallow and absorb and erase the horrid imprint of the unfortunate lesson - man's over-reach and laziness. Nature at the ready to make a century's long erasure of the presumed artifact of humanity, Oregon; both her broth of cleansing and her broil of render.

There were ten of us in the graduate painting program at the University of Oregon in swamp town. With names to make an author sweat with anxiety; names like Ferrari, Kaul, Lambert, Moulton, and Herman. One boring evening we sat encircled forced by Okada to talk about what shapes we saw to our futures. Did we, could we, envision a life beyond our graduate degrees?

One of us spoke of the need to get to London and push the boundaries of minimalism, for London was seen as the replacement for New York.

Another, under a haze of psychedelic stutter and ooze shrouded in Balkan Sobranie smoke, swore allegiance to Berlin as the coming epicenter of the arts.

Others fuzzed and fuddled about New York, LA, Seattle and all answers seemed to redirect the question to 'where do you see yourself planted?" Not "what do you see for yourself?"

My turn and I said "out here, in the coast range, someplace raising sheep and painting."

"Don't you get it man? This is no longer the sixties. It's 1971 and there is a future and it should be of your own making. Don't be a stupid romantic. You'll be left behind and sheep shit is all you'll know. Come with us man."

For that is how they saw it, they were all going together each to a different setting thousands of miles apart, but the sense was that this was a collective effort. They could not see it as the suicide that it was to become. They were visitors and leaving was their only option. Some of us were explorers not visitors and the intoxicating and regenerative rotting and germinating landscape offered, every day, glimpses into slow boil travel to flavors and shadings ready to give us each new shape. Oregon was not a place to go, to struggle within and be indentified with like New York City. Oregon was a place which married you to circular Pacific times and edible signature, you had here chance to exceed yourself to rhapsodic and shaping thrug. As they might say, "I don't know where he's from or where he lives now but he seems Oregonian." Maybe it's that his chameleon-like posture mimics the shape of the trees and rocks he stands near. When he's at the ocean's edge it appears that the spray passes through him as does the wind-thrust dust in the high desert. You get the sense he's punctuating the landscape with his posture and his readiness. You don't ask who he is, just as you don't ask who that homeless man is on the corner. Do you ask to know about that big rock or Juniper tree off to the side? No, because you don't care, you're just visiting. Oregon was a place you traveled within - not to - not from - but within.

If the young soldier, having survived his upbringing comes to murmur "now to make something of myself, now to take this cigar-shaped promise and blow it forward to the tower of statued promise" - he leaves as if stepping off the moving train that is that place to find himself rolling sideways past an imagined and on into the deep pocket of unnecessary reboot.

Our bargains do shape us. The conscious trade-offs - this velvet coat for that bag of rhyming marbles, these anxious friends for less friendly anxieties, the beekeeper's route for the nickle sandwich, the tortured thin brush for the aluminum foil scraps, these routines for Soutine's nightmares, the buttoned wasitcoat for the left flip-flop with gummed traction, the knowledge of imagined schedules for the dreads of the uninvited: these are the big bargains which malign spirit and they always prove to be bigger than they are. It is the tiny tradeoffs we sign up for which often reward us with corrective tissue. We choose to be here in harmony though it means we must remove our shoes. Oregon is that place which rewards us, with the space of mind, to mitigate all compromise, where the arrogance morphs to humor and the man wears shoes over shoes over shoes over socks painted to look like shoes over feet painted to look like furred paws over anklets of copper and manila braided to honor the psychosomatic well-ness dream. Oregon where convenience is allowed to stink. She, this throbbing landscape Oregon, will, in good-time, shed the mass of visitors - shake them loose as a dog shakes loose the sudden bath. She, this pickling forest clime, will walk out from under the temporaries and restake herself in preparation for the new gardeners, for the few careful farmers, for the life-giving wombs and fertilizing funeral pyres. She will shrink and cover, swell and hover, until all who neighbor avoid her social insolvencies and osmotic veneer. Oregon will always be a destination unachievable, unarriveable, lest the seeker be naked of self or selfish of his nakedness.

Cinco

What had any of this to do with farming?
Let me come to that in my own best way. Or not.
I 'sar' a movie tonight full of settling scenes and words that co-

alesced around surprising meanings, and a plot - oh my what a plot
- and it was clear immediately that such a fine thing had to come
first from a pen and I slipped to sadness in the complete knowledge
that a pen is no longer an instrument for all, it has become a dalli-
ance for those few who hold to their own returns - audience all of
a piece. The writer mustn't write to be read. The writer must write
to be surrounded by the surprise of what he has done. Just as the
farmer mustn't farm to feed people, he must farm to be surrounded
by the surprise of what he has done.

Seis

Atmospheres connect over memory's time, these connections
form temporary flyways shared by parallel flights of the amoebic
spirit. We pass ourselves coming and going. St Augustine's confusions, Rabelais' bounce, Humboldt's dread, Carlos Fuentes with
American cheese in his pockets, Gustaf Sobin's collection of pig
snouts, Bishop Tutu's tootoo. When all that is just out of sight it is
far more than what we see, know and trust but seldom more than
we are capable of feeling, that is the time of earned want.

I feel my childhood, struggling parents apportioning food at the
dinner table so all would have some. Never knowing new clothes.
Each of us holding, to our core, varying degrees of injustice. The
only sharing came of accidents. For our curious family love was
seen as weakness, we obeyed, we did not love. No shared secrets, no
team efforts, no traditional bonding. It made of us emotional curios,
freaks. On the surface we were each racers - not to beat one another
but to leave one another as far removed as we might. We had very
little other than shared space in an envelope of time. And that was
in spite of the poverty which might have brought us together. It was
because of our parents, so aloof, strangers to one another, and to us.

Yet providing, always providing, as we returned ever again to hungry cold days, always a solution came. Frugality, and its ugly cousin cold disdain, pulled us through but the colors and the beauty were missing. Pulled through we came to believe we always would be, that low as it was, a respite would come. False bargain. Beneath we came to our own that the only entitlement was life's want for inertia. Everything pushing in a current until the explosion of the fade.

We grew up as periphery's people, incarnate apologies for the discomfort we caused those guilty of their accidental affluence.

The crippled, wounded, dying, frightened, shared the waiting rooms with those of us poor who stood tight against the corners, hands deep in empty pockets, brains fogged.

And then to this one came glimpses of beauty's ticket, if we can understand the travelling of it. Tools became insanely important. Tools, including the push of skill. Tools including the interuption that is clarity.

It may be late in this old goat's life but I would like to own a pair of glasses which fit squarely on this crooked visage. Ah, to find a frame with cable ends, the frame itself of which allowed the "perispomenos," the bend around or the "circumflex."

An adoloscent; I found myself drawing pictures and those actions attracted surprised people who came insisting I draw something for them. It was as if what I drew, or the drawing itself, became a ticket or a pass to a better place, not for me - not for the artist - but for the priest, for the banker, for the brokers, for the boss, the councilman, for the controller - they needed passes and watching something of beauty be born of nothing was for them a pass they might steal, a way into heaven as much as a glimpse. It had to come observed, and only from a child's hand, from a perceived innocent. (Later in life I would learn the nearly parallel truth, that inconvenient humor in the form of a comical pet and/or mischievious grandchildren also provides glimpses into heaven.)

The cleverest in power came to understand that gifted children had to be coopted or sarificed lest they usurp. They were the ones who could steal from us our moment of borrowed clarity, of confusing calm, of powerful helplessness.

My empty stomach ached itself into knots and screamed 'me first' but my emptier heart usually won out, for the choice between trading heaven's pass for food or friendship always went to the fragile embrace.

And one unheralded day you find yourself granted the larger bargains, standing alone but befriended by your appreciations, your casserole of survivals and atmospheric authority. You find yourself capable and remembered to all of nature, for you have ridden the wider circles and jiggered the torn upholsteries to presumptive attention. All this while wearing on your nose the tatoo of 'volvement' the tatoo which announces 'I've arrived but I'll never be there yet.

Siete

Say something clever, she said... show them how smart you are. He gets it from his father, you know.

Later we would both learn that my cleverness did not belong to her. My cleverness was a key which got me into places I did not belong; from the circular sentences to accidental rhymes, youth may claim - maturity does so at greatest risk.

The priest at the commonwealth church had a curious pregnant eye when he asked if I, a twelve year old, wished to deliver a sermon before the entire congregation. He was certain he had delivered a 'lesson' with his question.

His mouth held open for a while when I said, sure.

What would you speak of?

Oh, maybe about how difficult it is to know what is right.

And, he asked, would you, could you support your words with scripture? Because I cannot at this moment imagine any passages which speak of such - what is right is obvious and known to us all.

I said nothing.

He with raised eyebrows thought to end the discussion with the ultimate challenge "then let's say Sunday evening next after vespers, you shall have the pulpit for twenty minutes. Ok?"

Sure, I said, seeing myself peering over the mahogany box and explaining agnosticism to the lost. Twelve years old.

I was offered a lesson, a whipping in the form of certain humili- ation, a come-uppance, a week's worth of terror in anticipation. But none of that happened. I wrote up a piece, let my mother dress me and plaster my hair and in 1959 I took my girl-hungry cock-sure self to that podium. I remember lots of faces, most looking fright- ened for me. I listened to my prepared words as they flowed from me without constraint and I felt the failing of my arguments, so I raised my eyes from the paper and spoke fresh words in pursuit of the idea in my brain. I saw people leaning forward waiting for the next thought. I had to be asked to step down, having gone over the time. The priest-come-minister seemed surprised and displeased.

You have a remarkable boy there, the man said to my mother.

She said nothing for she knew in that instant that I was a dangerous stranger and the worst sort of chattal. I was half human and half ulcerated undirected ambition. She lived fifty years more prepared for the humiliations she was certain were next. I was, to her, vermin.

And so in arrogance, Taking Man came to talk and talk and talk.

Ocho

I ask myself, before the congregation, what of Nicodemus and why we have the fear of Thomas? In the words of a twelve year old, if these things are right, which things are wrong? For every opposite needs have the elasticity of its bone-in contradiction. No, not the curse of relativity, it is specificity as the gift of voice to slipping innocence.

Ask ourselves does the argument have music? Does the argument come infused in the meringue of invitation? And the carriage of it all, need it be familiar or ascending in its strangeness? Complexity the bargaining coat? Simplicity the revealer? Is a thin wisp of a thing all lie? Are the suggestions of an unquantifiable thicket all deception? Is the chameleon a liar and as such 'wrong'? Is the law-perfect banker right and good? Why is justice never enough? Why does nature never allow measurements of right and wrong, only gone and done? "Love hurts, but justice is not enough." If Camus was right, murderous thug that he was, God's image must be thrum not man. If the lies and distortions of Cezanne and Matisse are righteous beauty, inescapable in their complexity, redoubtably deciduous in their charm, are we to jump little jumps, fist pumping and insisting wrong, wrong, wrong?

As we watched at every turn for blood, the indicating blood, no thoughts of right enter the worry. "Stop it!" we cry. We record extinctions, it is how we relieve ourselves. But in the presence of extinguishing, in the presence of last gasps, in the room with thedying we are at a most useless loss for action, for apt entry, for benediction. To make, with limber joints, the figure eight overhead requires a nude sense of apology's impermanence, an amorphous sense of the awkwardness of socio-biology, and an embrace of stupidity's burgeon. Where in any of this does right announce itself as stable, necessary, undeniable and useful?

A twelve-year old may feel these things as oily, vast, and insistant. But he cannot tell them from shit - unless he can, and then he finds he must explain that stuff out, lest he become an ever-circling human barber-pole of caution, of denial, of crispy.

A seventy-year old, if able, looks back over the trails of meaning and, if lucky, feels the memory of every old dog he stroked and every dead-too-soon child he loved and any question of righteousness makes him stinking, spitting, glaring, usefully mad.

Parables demand brackets, separate and low, slow starts. They want to be given the best chance to survive. They want the snap of bad times to assure their relevance. They do not want to be stupid in barber chairs and porch swings. They want a seated audience and the necessary sweetness to allow them to crawl into brains and swell.

We have the bad times and worse each day. The twelve-year old boys spoke in good and bad times with no such concern. They spoke in stories because they instinctively knew the long contradictory abuse of metaphor was essential. But they could know very little of the arbitrary rules of form. No long-fingered teacher had yet admonished them to 'do it all right or not at all!' That would happen with mixed juice when they turned thirteen, when in half-light they became attractive to themselves and feared they might blow it by being stupid.

Save us, Oh Lord, from the views of stupidity, for it does draw us to the cliff.

The seventy-year old wishes to have his presence felt after he has left the room.

The twelve-year old doesn't have a clue what that means.

Nueve

The age of twelve. If this is a narrative to be read, must it tie together neatly at points throughout with occasional summary conclusions? I want to believe not. Even to ask as much is to belie the initiative of this 'Talking.' It remains fiction; how thin is for others to decide, though doubtless few will find sufficient import here.

'Talking Man' is at its core, about the flow of sure words, something which requires armature. Form is not part of the chosen armature. Sirens in concert are. Splayed stories are. Compote may be a way to think of the conclusion. But we aren't talking Caribbean or Norwegian or Chinese or American or Sudanese or French. We are talking stew with the elasticity of marmalade, the pungency of anchovy paste, the heft of hog swill. And this with its own self-generating crust.

Discovered is hollow before time. 'Discovered-upon' is time before during and after. To be the 'discoverer' is to give every Aegean, every bright canyon, every numbered forest, every Bogata, its tenuous mooring. To be 'discovered upon,' to allow to be discovered upon, is to maternalize. To discover is to precauterize arrogance and greed. To leave the discoverable undiscovered is splendid, generous and the highest form of the regenerative. So to be the preemptive discoverer, to get only so close as to assure suspicion and then to hold tongue forever, to know from the quick shadow that the trophy fish indeed exists in the small hidden pond, to know this and to expend happy energy hiding the trail out is to lend the paternal the grace of perpetuity.

Only the bleeding greed, the bloody arrogance, shall be permitted ship-board. It would be scenery to carry an ounce of poetry forward through the sanguinity of failed 'inquiring' humanity. Portraiture and the stillness of life, where's the 'chalance,' got to hide it, there is no movement? Plastered boastings.

The twelve-year old boy was a result of instinct to the fore. "They smiled at me - and they did not care." Try that for a few years and find yourself asking "what's wrong with this picture?" You learn to protect yourself by first holding your own smiles - and then tentatively by offering a facsimile of a smile in exchange for...

Find the scripture for that, Carlton, and you've found leakage. Give me a holy book with leakage and my certainy will waft happily in the breeze of time's escape. I hear giggles.

Diez

In those earliest days there were the two dark conflicts. The constant prediction of pending death and the wide unknowable expanse to run through, no cover, no help, only limitless time. Now we run backwards, watching where we've been for answers to it all and missing the fast approaching horizon, horrible and beautiful in its exploding washes of color. Arms outstretched we catch truest life, some of it old and reflected.

Once Ounce Onse Eleban

My waking brain saw a formula for health, all physical, engaged, out away from the hollows of the mind, this as an old man.

Awake at twelve years old, before daylight, I found on the front steps a trussed bundle of newspapers. Walked my bicycle around to the front with a heavy, large, canvas bag hanging from high swooping handle bars. These gooseneck bars because I was someone ahead, someone who might someday be grand, someone announcing himself with effectiveness, someone who made of diligence an arching unquestionable stylishness, all while being painfully young. Mediterranean, sad, worker-child, floating his time presence. Gooseneck handlebars and Levi jeans. Shirt cuffs rolled up. Hair greased. A pouting pinch-eye scowl.

I sat on the steps each morning and folded those newspapers down into hard origamied squares that, when flipped just so, sailed to waiting yards and porches.

While this congested, lower-middle class ghetto of Los Angeles slept, I pedaled and tossed papers. Dogs barked, otherwise it was all my space. Empty, tired, otiose, repetitive, yet cinematic in odd new ways mixing the slippery promise of plastics with fat frying. In every direction, for as far as the eye could see, evidence of people stacked inside buildings, stacked inside city blocks, stacked, stacked, stacked, and blinking without rhythm. Concrete, asphalt. In the manner born, here it did not mean *'no thing authentic,'* all things short-lived, sincerety a broken goblet - it did mean for some the absolute essential of escape.

The boy could only escape through persistence. He knew he had to get up in the darkness, no matter the hour, fold those papers tight, no matter their thickness, pack his bag and pedal. He had to think hard and precise. Follow the exact same street pattern and never miss a house. He had to pitch the paper on to the porch or the steps or walkway, never on the grass and never to make a thump against the door, window or wall. His future and his paltry income depended upon it. It was rehearsal for escape and for life.

And this other boy of the suburbs (multiply him times one hundred thousand) he also looked around in that tight time before animal hungers and doubts beset him and for those days or weeks or months had only the close familiarities for comfort. If he was one of the fortunates he would pedal hard for pockets of aloneness and stare into space, into dark textures, into moving water, deep into himself. Not so much looking for answers as looking for a sign of the next steps. Without the paper route or the cows to milk he might accept the first thing shoved in his face.

My glorious own paper route and those hope-giving few coins it gave me - they were mine. No one else knew the moving line of that bicycle route before light, at first light, where the silent killer-dog's head would jam through in deafening snarl just as you passed. Only I knew that the new paint on the one house was the wrong color, hard to look at. And that occasionally unknown cars would leave the neighborhood before light. That the orange cat was entirely too big and that skunks and raccoons lived, just before light, in with people. And that those people were not prepared for that knowledge and unwilling to listen to the dogs, which tried to tell them about it - and that happens every darkest morning except that one where all animals went silent as a man's shadow moved in quick darts between buildings along fences and through bushes. The sight of the moving shadow, and the hollow silence, had been the only thing to ever stop me from pedaling, only thing to confuse my route, only thing about my job to make me mad.

The police came to the neighborhood the next day and stayed too long. I kept to my room until my mother came in cursing in Spanish and rummaging violently through my chest of drawers. In the cigar box she found the coins I had saved from my paper route - she seemed disappointed but took them all anyway and screamed at me that I was a thief and the bum, the *hibarjo*, she knew I would ever be. I was forbidden to leave the room.

Too many such experiences had piled up. I had no reasonable option, and since I had just turned thirteen, I had license so I went out the window and down the road. Gave up everything, including my paper-route, to walk and hitch-hike seventy-five miles to Paris, California, to start my life over with a clean slate.

We've heard this all before. Its truths come stale to our ears. Its leaves have fallen off and rotted on the ground. And none of that helps those new young boys avoid the first terrible false words shoved into their dark waiting holes.

Dose   Doze   Doce   Dulce

For some, time leaves ruts early and deep and unavoidable. For others, time reshapes and defines slowly and with new beauty at every stage. Goodness is oft thought to aid definition in time. But the correlation comes of wishful thinking. There is no correlation only sugaring which requires lessening if it is to have the weights of sincerity on its side. Every single damn one of us worries and analyzes too terribly much. The false promises regulary rearrange us. Hard work leading to success? Phooey. Decency leading to happiness? Careful planning to best outcomes? The value in those false promises rests in every beginning and sustenance - seldom in outcome.

We go not to have went but to be going. Getting there is pivot not posit. Without the brain rotating and sparking, a two cylinder magneto, all effort transpires inertia - flutters, spurts, and stalls. We may think too much in the trough of the stall but never too much just ahead of the zenith.

They say at a year and a half, in Rio Piedras, Puerto Rico, I crawled out an upstairs doors and gazed down concrete steps to a watermelon below. Before anyone could stop me, I fell and rolled to the bottom. No one thought to consult a doctor. Before this I was a happy baby, after I cried incessantly and was sequestered in dark rooms away from my black-haired mother who could not stand the noise and yelled to anyone that I did it to shame her. She was pregnant with one of my brothers. She suspected him, as she did me, only long before he was born.

Ten years later, on physical exam, a doctor determined I had broken my collar-bone in that early fall and it had healed crooked.

Sixty years later, xrays revealed I had broken my neck in that same early fall and the vertebrae had healed in a nerve-pinching lump.

All that from the fall. The worst pain was having a mother who completely disowned me and worked to have me shamed and away from her.

Now I understand how a precocious twelve year old might feel entitled to ask a congregation from the pulpit - how can we know what is right and what is wrong? God's divination, so often categorical, carpets society, carpets the mass not the solitary. God's divination seldom blends with mercy and never offers understanding of exception.

God is the math in the pattern.

The Entire Abbreviated Second, Second Half of the Book

Anyhow

No training wheels, no guidelines, no turn-overs, not a single outside anticipation in sight. The roll continues with hapless the standard, and easy decency the wardrobe.

The story of this talking man splays across the pages in search of chronic infection and the occasional comic arrogance.

Up close is where it has always mattered most. In a moment of sweet reverie, knee a whisker from the sound-system speaker, I could feel a vibrating whisper to match the bass line of the song and a deepest positive hum. That's when you know your ground is tight and solid against the frame, as the electrical charge of all time and God's supreme indifference waves through you without harm, without interuption.

The impatient fellow asked "Must you breath so hard? What's wrong with you? And you mumble and grunt to yourself all the time. That's not who you are. Can't you make an effort?"And you smile the vapid smile. He has absolutely no grasp of what it means to play to yourself. Nothing you say in response can have the heft of his interuption or the slice of his cut. So you, eyes cramped, say nothing and in that simple way the contact is broken, disposed of and all is lost except for the sweet affirming loneliness.

You change the color, you change the feeling, you change the sound, you alter the memory, you change the taste, you go elsewheres, you just might merge with an entirely new flow. The nerve-melting power of distance when what biology needs is top growth that waves, with heritage, to the future. Tides, times and useful tatters never at war with metamorphosis, there in we find vitality and the balancing songs of universal math.

But any of this from an old man on the steep seems useless to a garbage degree. There are days like this when remembering the source stories would help, but the sort of strength and internal curiousity it takes isn't there. The ways back in are sensory - I remember entire times of this history had their own flavors, and smells are flavors to the open brain, the brain waiting to grow and shape, the brain beginning to identify what it did not want. It did not want the plastic emptiness, the odorless order, not even the Avery Brundage museum purities. So afraid of light and dust. The brain wanted those working clutters that bespoke lovely process - there was that hauntingly beautiful steam-powered sawmill deep in the shades of the California redwoods, oily in its burble and hiss, forceful in its push and pull, fragrant from the forest intimacies and all married to the best biologies.

Pity the laziness.

As a poor child I learned to play simple games that have served me well for a very long age. Pick-up Sticks: an example. Hold a handful of toothpicks, the longer the better, and set them down, end first, on the table. Release them. With only one stick as a tool, very carefully remove each stick without moving any of the others. Alternate until someone moves a stick and is forfeit.

Now I find myself trying to carefully reconstruct the pile that has been my life, one stick at a time but understanding the implicit reverse fiction in the process. So many elements which power forward but remain invisible; the smiles, the fears, the loves, the hungers, the pains - none of these concrete enough to be structured and yet each powerful and elemental.

Painting has been a way for me, and others, to 'capture' those intangible elements, at least at their essense, and hold all they create as energy. The urgencies and restrictions have prevented me from painting, these last several months. All of the past times painting have given me strength and a borrowed calm. Same with music. I protect my insistence that I will return by revisiting the incompletions of this life.

Married at twenty-one for no good cause, and drafted to be a bartender for the Scarpula/Alioto family of San Francisco. If Lou Diamond Phillips could parlay Phillipine heritage to native american film roles why not, long before that, a Puerto Rican mulatto molded into an Italian bartender? Nineteen sixty-eight began in the restaurant kitchen of Tortola's learning at a service bar how to mix drinks. Over the previous two years there were bouts with commercial fishing, woodcutting and farmhand work all stirred in with painting and art school - the best part of which was working in the Art Institute basement art supply store for Roberto Quagliata while listening for the artifical heartbeats of Grace Slick,

The memories of that time have a tortoise-shell-as-jewelry quality; the sheen, the wood-grained hopefulness, the sharp-edged refusal of the totemic. The way it hides that it has been carved. Its false *brittalia*. The portal which divides the sensorial memories of childhood from the first satisfactions of adult hungers is framed in invisible caramel-colored, deeply grained, fractured tortoise-shell - the sort for which no tortoise gave its life - the sort which required best imaginative description - the sort which give garage test-tube tinkers blended hope.

Obituaries of the living lend quickened rust to history. Obituaries of the recently passed ogre (not auger) sadness, forgive unforgivables, and flatten horizons that never existed. (I don't know the particular daily scope and bottomless sacrifice of my son's journey but I see its deafening tone.) When we tell the story hungry for its impactful conclusion do we give directions? Or is it a filter in itself that screams "stay on task!"?

The best toast? "Anyhow."

We fear to say. The planet heaves, shudders, heats, races to its peril, to a threatened end and the humans bring it all on, invest themselves in horrid angst over transexual toilets and adequate electricity for cannabis growth: massive hunger and poverty and doom for a third of her kind and humanity spits about what? Flexible LCD screens and retina cameras kill the hearing of sight and the plight of sonority. Bartok never existed. Ernest Gold should have been compared to ____________ but never... When the focus tightens it is to moments squeezed from oddly colorful tedium.

Restaurant bartender, from kitchen service to front, back and forth, every night except one. Every Wednesday a limousine would deposit Joe DiMaggio for his ritual. Left side of the dining room, all booths vacated save for center for the *Yankee Clipper*. And he would permit no one to wait on him but me. Maybe it was because when he first met me he said, "Hey kid, you know who I am?" I had no clue but his hang-dog horseface seemed a signature. I wanted to answer with a question and ask "Hey old man, you know who I am?" But instinct said "be afraid of this one," so I said "No sir." He glared and laughed; one of the only times. From then on it was understood, no one else would serve him in that restaurant. So every Wednesday I was to stand at attention and heed his every demand.

Ernest Gold was a brilliant composer who squeezed from cinematic tediums the truest songs of things, people, moments. His theme for Exodus, the movie, was melodramatic, soaring, sour and splendidly evocative of modern epic and tragic comedy. Not unlike Joe DiMaggio. But who cares. The world slides to our doom and who cares? In 1968 Joe DiMaggio didn't care. He had tied himself to his own cage and angrily waited his end. Our end or ends did not matter to him. His specifics, so large - grandiose even - no longer mattered. He was an old, tired, circus bear who knew exactly how to unsnap his tether but would never do so. On Wednesday our game would play out: Compari on the rocks or DuBonnet - always either, twist my arm at the wrist until it hurt then push me away. Yells, glares, insisting on the other always the other. When I thought I'd be smart and have both ready and near by, it drove him nuts - he stormed out. Thought I'd be fired but Fran said "he loves you kid. You give him the kinda attention he's gotta have." Huh?

Just as every writer craves a reader he can smell, feel, try to second guess: can you see when that reader is listening, is watching, for what's to come? In the case of the Talking Man the reader is the past, we feel it in the gearing - the whirl like a failing bendix until the alignment is true and gears mesh to make the movement proper - but only for a split second then it falls away like a weak spring until the next test, the next machine reading, the next sorry *gullibrated* vibration of instinct pushes out more words - words about things, words strung together in a necklace ringing time's dinner bell.

DiMaggio, turning outside in, had few words only swimming images that soaked and yanked at him. He was exhausted, a fire fighter of his own life, he sat and swatted at his thoughts. If he found indifference he caught it and slapped at it occasionally to feel he had a little control over that small piece of his time.

Three years before, working as a box-boy and lady's shoe salesman at Leed's on Market Street, I shared infancies with Cornelius
Wise, a young black man of rare dirt purity. We worked side by
side, joked constantly, and used each other to break-in tentative
approaches to the mysterious back side of adulthood. No sound
when he laughed, body sucking in tight, shaking, shoulders pointing straight up. Smile so wide with surprise that it changed the
shape of his face. Infectious. Just as were all the indications that he
held in millions of delicious secrets. Wrinkles moving across his face
in spastic combinations with winks, head shakes and wobbles. In a
series, over many days, he shared the minutae of what was required
to please a woman. Great painstaking detail, yet, with time I realized
he told me nothing, only suggested masterfully with phrases like
"... you know man, they like it slow and you gots to go wide like a
swing and change right away, make em think you a snake and then
before they can catch der breath you need you to use yor 'spressions
to make 'em laugh. It's all close work man. You get it right and they
feed you, feed you for the longest time."

There was the Fillmore auditorium, Graham's bizarre culture
bazaar, and there was the Fillmore district, the black enclave. Cornie, itching to shake things up back home, took his light-skinned
mulatto brother to a Fillmore nightclub in '65 or '66. Set me up
with a blind date, beautiful black girl. Not far from the fillmore
auditorium, where most any night Big Brother and the Holding Co.
wailed with jumping Janis, we sat near the stage at a round table
in another dark smoky bar. Many heads turned in open distrust to
see someone so light skinned with a sister and in this sacred place.
Chairs scratched the floor to warn of things that might come. Then
clearing every passage way, as we worried and nursed whiskeys, came
a fanfare - curtain parted and four tall, thin, strikingly handsome,
arrogant black men, in matching pastel suits, strutted in perfect

dance step to the center singing in harmonies that defied gravity, that thrummed us down deep, spellbinding, Grecian, African, Jamaican, Detroitian. The harmonies swelled and echoed, swirling around meandered storylines that would have set fire to Billy Shakespeare's ear hairs. They called themselves the *Temptations* and my oh my were they.

Oh what divine secrets Cornie gave me to hide for my own wrinkle juice. I had those in my pockets when three years later Joe DiMaggio would throw his drink in my face and ask "What you smiling about punk?"

Gary Snyder had his Katmandu, I had my Frisco, the degrees of difference at this late stage - so much dried dead skin.

Supposedly.

Don't know where the image came from. It's tight in on the back corner of my mind cup. Clear. Definitive. They were big, upright, long-eared, black mules, probably Percheron-cross. Long, thin, perfectly proportioned legs reminded us of basketball players or large spiders. Well fed, round, glistening. Sad discerning eyes pretending not to care while seeing everything. In sparse harness, dirty canvas tubes over rusty chain traces. Two of them, certainly unidentical twins or the result of a mule man's long-years search for the match.

Standing there not an ounce of submission in the two postures. At attention yet relaxed like a newly promoted colonel. Something about the two said "you better get up before us if you want to be on the team."

Seventy seems old enough, just need time to secure the question

for family. Then there are days when seventy seems like just a beginning. Avoiding the shut-offs still the challenge. Such thoughts rob
from the swirl and flow of talking.

The black mules stood directly in front of the black-haired girls
and my sexuality shifted gently to the bohemia of wishful thinking
rather that the airstream of desperate wants.

Memories, out in the open, rigidify to a static depth of field.
While landscapes to the discerning eye fluctuate from near and
wide to far and thin. The explanations escape me. But those black
mules don't. I know they are always there just behind that big rock.
That's me using my memories to reach forward. Or maturity as a
souring agent. We wait anxiously for maturity, for the rewards and
membership it promises but it always arrives before we are prepared
and then it is too late. We bargain most of our lives for the mysterious, unless we are simpletons, and with age the satisfactions of the
simpleton comfort us. Napping in the presence of sunsets, throwing the ball for the dog, listening intently to the meander of a small
child, apologizing to yourself for yourself - comforts. As the loss of
hearing, sight and balance progress, the mirrors at the periphery go
clear and molten. Inside all brocade.

You may want to read here more of DiMaggio but I have no
need to write more of him. I do though love the sound of his name
and believe it should belong to a great painter or poet - DeMag-
ique - which brings this brain squarely onto the question of the
need for a towering novel of a strong, silent, creative person whose
artistic pursuits pile, and grow, and swell to staggering value, until
the world insists itself upon him and angers his blood. Through his
fragile innocence he escapes to fulsome loneliness.

Ah, but am I me?

The rule of law, and the need for justice are not reconcilable.

Sputter

If the law enforcement officials had broken into Albert Camus' apartment after his death and searched for clues as to his behaviour in the French underground, searched for evidence of his lifelong motives, what case might have they brought against him? Moralist? Murderer? Failed journalist? Essayist? Liar? Autobiographer? Petty Novelist? What would today's media do with the back stories of Kafka, Neruda, Hoffa, Stegner, Nabokov, Faulkner, Gaugin, or Stalin.

Rewrite above.

Sputter

Context: one person's exotic - one person's ordinary - humans have less inter-species commonality than any other life form. Schadenfreud and candied terrors.

Sputter

Sixty years past the haunt of the black-haired girl, the talking man watches from his booth of separation as mankind's embrace of "hyper-kinetic connectivity" (not my words - don't want them) has given each human a device that tells it or him what to do, where to go, what to get excited about. And people 'gather' to be subsumed or slaughtered or digested for their collective energies. Makes a mockery of all those precise equations of unsustainable energy consumption and envrionmental degradation to see how "soft ware" destroys us all at such a meteoric rate. A case can be made that humanity will not be in attendance for the "short" coming.

Sputter and festering bluster

Can't seem to hold to what I know to be true: never look over your shoulder - always look over your shoulder - trust in outcomes -don't trust in outcomes.

Bluster

"How come I don't know you? Never heard of you or your work? It's not possible to do a lifetime of work of this quality and be completely unknown, invisible, unheard of?"
There is a great pained beauty in all of this. Massive disconnect pointing towards ever greater sincereties.
And that story-teller who owns lies so completely he creates of them staggering beauty and loads of quivering laughter. He is still insolvent, he is ultimately but colorization of the problem. For, as the end would approach, it is he who will reach incoherence and incontinence first.

Portrait of the artist as a tortured nucleus? Striving to make the case through narrative and meander, that artistry is not so much the result of environmental circumstance as it is the nature of its survival; survival of that time and trial. How did he survive? What did it take and where did it take him?
But there can be no denying that something came before the beginning. I so clearly recall at ten years old feeling the "complete" marvel and energy from my first drawings and paintings - that these things might come out of me with a "pre-wind."
But the black-haired girl/woman could not allow the revelation.

Her soul depended on her soul being the source, and that glorious thing had to be something less than her. She had one requirement - that I beg always for her approval while aknowledging that any and everything I made or could do came from her. At each and any inkling that what I was, am, would be, might be beyond her reckoning, the bitterness and disregard grew.

And when I could no longer feel her, see her, owe her, she disappeared and I emerged.

Artist of the portrait as a nucleur torture

"Hello"
I sat down, uninvited, at her table.
"I wrote the book you are reading."
"Why should I believe you?"
I opened my wallet and set it on the table.
"Seventy years old?" said with just a trace of dismissal, she frowned and the moisture on her cheeks dried in place.
"I just wanted to know which part made you cry?"
"What? I'm not crying. This is so weird."
She got up, dropped the book and left.
So now, I will never admit to having written anything ever again.

When the writing is out ahead, ahead of insistence, ahead of complicity it must survive the fire - stay afloat - avoid the dismissals - so it does. When the writing follows behind, being insisted upon, complicit in the author's idiocies - it burst into ash, chokes the waiting fish and shits out the dismissers ass.

The disparities between the terrors of night and the assignments of day are so vast as to invite schizophrenia.

Hide your complexeties - the restituioners are near.

As a decorated agnostic, I stand before you, God's secret control for the high speed experiment and less obvious research into a lasting significance.
Does criticism come roaring when missed opportunity, so blatently exposed, forces confessions thinly disguised?

Hot water slowly over the hands brings the cold interior to a borrowed refresh. It is a moment.

It is impossible for there to have been a time that this beast, which is human, existed without words, without language. Even now, some of us reach back before our own amniotic fluids to a time of words in perfect harmonic balance. We are not advanced, we are advancing to...

We tire of the stories of past experience and we know them to be carriage towards the bag. But the bag? It diminishes as it goes out and down; it is just a moment and the values are shelved and the bag is burnt. Is this the reason we don't want to hold the magic? Is this the reason we turn to reason, that mathematical accounting reality which forces absolute balance from the crazy fertility of life? Time, calendars, speeds, sound, light, love, anger, bliss, none of these things "balance" out. None come to the "all accounted for." All spill out and away, as well as in. Suspense accounts and leap years, all factored to explain away the unexplainable.
The shop stewards of the new Babylon, plexiglass clipboards and laser pencils in hand, dope-slapped to hand-off distracted lies, they

are paid by commission for each rubberized *gullibrated* soul they deliver. Shakepseare's secret was the defining force of the Globe theater - without it he become a simmering simper. There are defining forces which reside and shape entirely from within the individual intellect. Many painters come to mind.

This man, so completely immersed in dread and fear, incapable of maintaining an open appreciative outlook, balancing his own destruction, who is to say what brand of coward? Once he was a juggler and friend, an adventurer and a locksmith - what is he now? A loose end, a bit of fray, nobody's proud moment? His artistry stripped from him, his handlings gone, he wants to be but the wasting of terror boils his remaining vitality which thickens to the edge of death.

Borrows from 7-16: I stink on you, you filthy wonder.

...and we still need to hold on to the physicality of what we've done, what we know and how we work. For the electronics may not survive in the next times; how we feed, warm and house ourselves, how we store foods, how we power ourselves, how we seed ourselves, forward through time, how and where we store the books that hold the clues? How we perceive? Rules of grammar, synchronicity, age, appetites, eyes; they each are quandrous. Their relevance stupid with old clothes, assumptive at most elbows, hiding the rot, and helpful at many a turn.

Eyes, take eyes. How we, through ours do perceive they, through theirs and assign depth, shallowness, import, kindness, evil and imbalance?

We toxic snobs, we forgettable brights, we late to the party early to embarassement pocket thumbs, we have nothing offerable.

It is long past time to break with computers. The conundrum is that humanity in its current sorely abbreviated form resides in that electro-syrup universe. I want to talk to you but you aren't anywhere to be spoken with. Even here, you aren't here.

Not as Beethoven is *here* in his *Cavatina*.

Sleep and hunger. Sleepy and hungry - cousins of transition, of transport, of apology. Pathways open to next states but also states in and of themselves, where reality pings. The sonars are deep set in our genetic code. And genetics need protection Manipulated, they fail to answer the ringing pinging questions of tired and of hungry. No code, no instinct, no paths forward. Mankind readies itself for the erasure of life's greatest and most vital mysteries. As the bankers and brokers laugh and stroke their new automotive leathers, all of nature - mankind conflated - awaits genetic erasure. The wild dogs, the cockroaches, the ants and crows they hold for the next incarnations. But will the carrion of clones and mutants drain away all unexlainable motivations?

We, each of us, allow the edits from our periphery; those who step up, between the energies, and mention, jab, and cajole us to inflate, deflate, and erase, they are the thieves. Once I thought they only existed with legitimacy, daring formation and fomation - that with maturity came the unfettered times - but I was right. Now as age and life's morphology strip me, the editors have gone and I am allowed to spew. Where is the usefulness in that? Where does our next hurrah come from? Does the talking man have rights to reach back to the new young ages where care is so illusive?

The clamming (as in clam shut) influence of this blistered widening time kills tradional motivations. What any one person has to say or show matters less and less. The colors we painters bring into each gray are eliminated by color management systems designed for digital ease. The way in which strings of words might continue, over

all time, to burn their relevance into the host sheet, allowing meaning and the colors of thought to splay out across the curved screen
of a living reader, this is the got-chalk truth God would keep in his
armpits for men are still to young to handle it.

I know and have known that these books, written in the longest
of long hands contain and protect the magic. It has never been and
never will be in the computer which is at best a short-lived conveyance and plastic service for the mind. Faster? Perhaps but where to?

And these graphite pencils and fountain pens insist on displa-
ing the evidence of thoughts, trips, drips and hollows. The magic
releases the light, sometimes correctly.

I will offer up decoration and wide vision and neighborly distance with tired humility. I give them permission to disregard me
and all that remains is paper ash.

So where does talking man go? To mumbles and scofflaw? To
talking into a bag? To feeling the breath of talk bounce back from
the close-in alley wall?

Deniability and the dry heaves of "it just doesn't matter." We go
forward to the suspension bridge of stringy fears and wonder just for
a small moment whether the other side is different? How did we not
see the rationales all bunch to make a bad choice be the only choice?
How did we not see our scntribution to the moral insolvency of our
time?

My other voice says to me, "you deside when the end-game is
upon you - you decide." And I argue with myself to say "so long as I
refuse to consider an end-game, my flow continues to ancient Japa-
nese thickets of bamboo and next passion." The loaded brush, three
colors full, rolls it mark to the sounds of surprised sighs.

Some men when they close their eyes receive dark, thick and
quiet. Some transition to crazy patterns, invasise lights, screaming.

Some enter another universe, sightless and either emboldened or frightened. We close our eyes to leave and to investigate. Where in that is rest?

Young, we are told our whole lives are ahead of us and we do not hear the gift of that. Old we may find the space of heart to wish to tell the young "your whole life is ahead of you," but well ahead we know the words will fall flat. So the sentiments rattle in our later beings, rattle like rocks in a slow rotating hubcap. And the young gather in circles of thirst and loneliness, angry that all the signs are vacuum. All save for music, poetry and painting - all else tells too much or too little, all in a wrinkled fistful of wrapper papers and empty oil bottles. Other evidence hides itself outside of measures of consequence, how the body and visage is shaped by years of passionate marriage to creative process. Joshua Bell's mouth, shaped by the press of chin against violin, the shape of Renoir's arthritis insisted upon the brush. Shakespeare's head in homage to the Globe theater.

All men, all women, tie back to the formative tether and the skins of nurture. We must be needed, or we refuse to be held. Or we fight both and spend it all to deny.

Portend emptiness,
hollowed borrow,
death the wither,
torn shirt, lost waivers
and forgiveness
the empty hand
up in the face.

go away they say
we are done with you.

pulling burrs from
inside weave,
spirit did not shatter
its membrane,
limp now,
flapping aggressive seeds
forming hull mail,
harrowing the skin of that farmer,
irrigating dustmud
with slow blood,
a paste for
another nest.

Some would simply end. And some would enter a swirl of protracted ending, healthier than prescribed, refusing sarcastic retirements, forcing the last flies of fall to lead us back to warm corners, forcing cosmetics past comedy and toward all excuses for youth, toward Egon Shiele's aversive 'plump' beauty. All sources raked into piles with those bloody seeds and manured teas of the righteous righteous.

Through to the other side save for now, we understand the slowest crucible of consequence. And in one hand there are mountains of the past to judge against the volcanos of this moment.

The third voice disappears when it is listened for. At the periphery I feel as much as see the large dark shape flit by. When I turn to look, it is only a bird dancing from branch to branch on the lilac bush out the window. That third sight has disappeared when it is looked upon, not the dark passing shape but the ability to see it. The seeing passes with looking. The dark 'imagined' shape is not important. The third sight is the bridge, is the passage, is the entry. But sight is only one, there are others: memory, hearing, scent, near-touch, longing, and purposeful movement.

Keeping that outside view, out of mind - in of feeling, denies the energies of precise calibration and welcomes the sought-after balance.

But balance requires imbalance without which there can be no counter-veiling. Perfect balance is precarious, it is an acting upon. It wants manifestation of the fiscal equivalency of mixed metaphor. How can it be this and that? The better question is, how can it not be?

Back to this memory: the soured salt, ocean scum of the Sausalito houseboat moorings kept in check by the windy Pacific mists suctioned into every corner of this most Italian of bays, most northern of bayous, most volcanic of Shanghais; even it could not compete with the draw of the mossy, sweet-creeked rainforests gummed with leaf mold and bear prisons. An away birth of the thin parable of the brilliant idiot.

winter frightens,
its shear weight
promise of deadening
hibernation
death

lumbering
incontinence
that other intelligence,
beauty
the spoon

Nobody expected you to read this far. I certainly didn't.

Its implicit. If you are a practiced story-teller you understand the promise that you will finish the story or never get another shot at it. These stories are strings still attached to the long ago, honeymoon bumper cans flattened or missing. The travel has frayed them and braided a few to a crazy tail of tales.

This thin fiction, brittle with lies, stories itself into those glorious spaces roiling over and under the chartable betweens.
One thousand times seekers came to this young soul and put themselves in view not to be seen, not to see, but to be allowed access and to what?

I have never sought portal. Does that make me one? If I am a door, may I ever know this?

Any distraction now releases thoughts like so many birds. You cannot catch those escaping thoughts, you must trust your patience that they will return and alight.

Cab Calloway, the manic jazz-dancing human grasshopper with fling-round coat-tails and retractable fingers, made of hisself a full-body carnival barker and happy elegy. He won, you know. No witch, no accountant, no predatory lender, no twisted mother could reach through the swirl of his understanding madness to grab him. He jumped with the little spiders, lept with the frogs, flapped with the teals, horseshoed hisself into laddered corners and greased tunnels. And he lubed it all with laughter.

Talking with ghosts is very much a meal of leftovers, we can go after them cold and casually, or we can 'ask' them to dinner with new onion, old curry, surprise additions. Molasses, raisins, girlee liqueurs and bacon fat will make ghosts and left-overs squeal forward in time. Old brain fog tests resolve, tests any ability to travel. To the grave with unreasonable insistence goes every internalized being. We keep ourselves out of the fog by seeing forward with our entire being, by using imagination as a fog claw. the claw does not tear away, it climbs through, it transports us to the view, clearest view, of the imagined. And, here be the wonderful secret, we model our actuality from the imagined. It is the modeling which sees us forward, which makes of us forward, which makes of us hopefulness, forward.

So what of young fog?
We live in a house built by drunken dwarves and added to by day-laborers with beer disease.

How long did you sleep asked the one.

"Don't know. Woke three times, once in darkness, once in light and once in tears."

Suffer me snobs; sausaged, blue-nailed, thought-thirsty, inside the order to die. Sun in my eyes as it aligns itself for the evening, walking through lush wet green grass and clover ten inches into second growth. Breeze a perfect backslap to the gentle warmth, I think of deepest interiors of race and of nationality, where love songs sauce insistence and play to longing's apology.

Rivers of frost, a tureen of casoulet, I'm sick and tired of the sick and tired. I'm a bio-spastic farmer with poor poetic tendencies. Everytime we are careful not to offend we miss an opportunity to plant a seed. Do not equate meanspiritness with truth, or decency with agreeability.

Afterwords

This book might be about one thing but it is meant to do something else altogether. The territories so thinly visited here, are my territories. You are not welcome to them. I did not set out to share, I did not set out at all. I sat here and cried onto these sheets because I could not shut up.

Now it is in a few hands and the trespassers invite themselves forward. I knew they would. So I marked the perimeter with the juice of my kidneys to cause pause. Magic must also be employed to keep trespassers at bay. The magic of the elongated and finger-rolled lie to draw the weasels amongst you far away, to seek those illusive archipelagos of the giant lizard harvest, as there you may do no harm.

Any good pig farmer knows, urination is God's gift to the alchemists of privacy. For privacy is gold. And the privacy of gold is made as much from vacuums and voids as it is from stockades. Urine (and pig is the strongest) creates the repulsing void which turns those wind-up toys towards the edge of the table and off ...

My brilliant, beautiful, long-suffering wife wrapped it up for me by observing, "You don't pee enough to make a difference."

There I did it.